APEX MAGAZINE SFFH

STRANGE. BEAUTIFUL. SHOCKING. SURREAL.

EDITED BY JASON SIZEMORE

I0517316

ISSUE #0: WINTER 2017

Jason Sizemore, Editor-in-Chief
Lesley Conner, Managing Editor
Bianca Spriggs, Editor
Hannah Ruth Krieger, Assistant Editor
McKenzie Johnston, Assistant Editor

Apex Publications, LLC
PO Box 24323
Lexington, KY 40524

www.Apex-Magazine.com

Available by subscription (www.Apex-Magazine.com) or through your favorite online vendor (Amazon, Barnes & Noble, etc.).

Cover art copyright Sunny Ray

ISBN: 978-1-937009-48-9

FEATURING:

John Hornor Jacobs

Nisi Shawl

Michael R. Underwood

Anton Strout

Alyssa Wong

Alethea Kontis

Adam-Troy Castro

Delilas S. Dawson

Maurice Broaddus

Kat Richardson

Ferrett Steinmetz

Rati Mehotra

Lucy A. Snyder

Shanna Germain

A.C. Wise

Keffy R.M. Kehrli

and many others!

"This compendium of literary undercutting and rebuilding is both enjoyable to read and an incisive work of commentary on the genre."
— *Publishers Weekly,* (Starred Review)

Upside Down: Inverted Tropes in Storytelling is an anthology of short stories, poetry, and essays edited by Monica Valentinelli and Jaym Gates. Over two dozen authors, ranging from NYT-bestsellers and award winners to debut writers, chose a tired trope or cliche to challenge and surprise readers through their work.

Read stories inspired by tropes such as the Chainmaille Bikini, Love at First Sight, Damsels in Distress, Yellow Peril, The Black Man Dies First, The Villian Had a Crappy Childhood, The Singularity Will Cause the Apocalypse, and many more...then discover what these tropes mean to each author to find out what inspired them.

ISBN TPB 978-1-937009-44-1

Apex Publications

ApexBookCompany.com

AVAILABLE IN TRADE ($18.95), HARDCOVER ($27.95), AND DIGITAL ($4.99).

WHAT SAY YOU?

WORDS FROM THE EDITOR-IN-CHIEF

Thank you for picking up issue 0 of *Apex Magazine SFFH*. Before you jump into our excellent selections of fiction, nonfiction, and interrogations, I wanted to take a moment to tell you what this is and what it's about. This primer should give you a good idea for those uninitiated Apex readers. This might read somewhat like a mission statement, but this is *issue 0*, so I think it is warranted.

We started out as a quarterly print journal back in 2005 as *Apex Science Fiction and Horror Digest*. After twelve issues, the magazine distribution system had beaten me up pretty good, so I dropped the print aspect and switched to digital only around 2009. This digital only version had a much simpler name: *Apex Magazine*. The digital zine is monthly. We're up to issue 92.

What you're holding is an experiment to answer a question. Will Apex readers be sufficiently interested in a dead tree edition of our online content to make doing one financially viable? I hear from a handful of readers at every convention I work that if the zine was printed, they would buy a copy. Certainly, a large percentage of people saying that are being polite and hoping it gets the desperate vendor off their back. But some of those people are being honest, right? Right? There is also the online fans who prefer the feel of paper on their fingers. While I love eBooks, I can empathize with that notion. After working in front of a computer monitor or digital table all day, I prefer to do my casual reading the old-fashioned way.

There are a few things you need to know about *Apex Magazine* and its editors.

We are unabashedly proponents of diverse literature. Our readers often tell me that one of the favorite aspects of reading our publication is that they never know what they're getting. While we do work strictly in the boundaries of genre fiction, we seek to publish content by people of all colors, sexual preference, race, gender, or any other definition of non-white cishet male. Don't misconstrue that as our editors actively opposing the work of white cishet men. Heck, we publish plenty of those guys. But we also want to publish voices that are underrepresented or underappreciated. Diverse fiction is interesting. Vanilla fiction is not.

We unabashedly skew toward dark science fiction, dark fantasy, and horror. While I'm an optimistic business man, I am pessimistic about humanity and technology. If you're looking for happy endings and sunshine, then we might not be the publication for you. We have a unicorn story starting on the next page. Aren't unicorns the epitome of innocence and purity? Author K.T. Bryski says "not so fast" and we adore her for it.

Finally, we unabashedly love our readers. We're always trying to please them. I often think we try too hard (for example, this magazine you're holding), but in the end, readers are worth it. Without them, there is no *Apex Magazine*.

I want to thank all the authors, artist Sunny Ray, and Justin Stewart for helping make this experiment happen.

Happy reading!

—**Jason Sizemore, editor-in-chief**

THE LOVE IT BEARS FAIR MAIDENS

K.T. BRYSKI

Warning: This story contains content that some readers might find disturbing.

The hunt begins as it always does: with quarry, bait, and hunter.

Let's see if we've got this right.

A young maiden settles herself in a sun-kissed glade. Sixteen, eighteen, never much older than twenty. Clover cushions her feet and gold-drop daffodils bob in the breeze. Maybe there's a stream burbling close by. There usually is.

Then—suddenly, silently—the creature steps from between two birch trees. The noble unicorn slips into our glade. Dark eyes blink; its dainty hooves don't even bend the grass. White fur shines like spun moonlight. It's the pony we all wanted growing up.

Except for the horn, of course. Long and spiralling, tapered to a sharp point. Maybe it's black, maybe white, or maybe even gold. It doesn't matter. What matters is that the horn is very long, very thick, and very hard.

Think about that for a moment.

So the unicorn steps towards our maiden, not looking anywhere else. Only at her. Like it's devouring her with its gaze. And our maiden, she doesn't even move. She barely even breathes. She sits there, frozen, her back ramrod straight as the wild animal draws closer and closer. Until its hot breath drags over her cheek, and its stench scours her nostrils. You know that reek. Dirt and musk and shit.

Sorry.

Excrement.

Our maiden still doesn't move. The unicorn bends its knees, preparing to put its giant head in the maiden's lap. You know, with the *long, thick, hard* thing a couple inches from her crotch.

Can we forgive the maiden for inhaling sharply and bolting through the woods, cold with terror?

See, here's the thing.

Unicorns are horrific creatures.

Look at them. We've got this wild beast that's mostly a horse, only with an ice pick on its head. Trust me: horses' hooves and teeth are plenty sharp. They don't need anything else.

Except a unicorn's not only a horse. It's a patchwork mess of the least attractive quadrupeds. Cloven hooves, like a goat—and Satan, incidentally, but the symbolism *there* would take a while to work through—and often the goat's beard, as well. Boar tail. Elephant feet. Stag heads. Sometimes they're actually just rhinoceroses.

I've never seen that in any tapestry. The gentle spring glade, delicate young maiden, and a rhinoceros barreling towards her. You'd run too, I bet.

Back to our maiden. She races through the trees. A shoe falls off, snagged on a root, but she doesn't break stride. She didn't know she could run that fast, but when you're desperate and scared, you can do a lot you never realized.

Hooves pound the earth behind her. Our maiden gasps for breath, glances over one shoulder. In the forest's treacherous light, she keeps losing sight of her pursuer. The unicorn is white in a dark forest, but that doesn't make it any less sly. It cloaks itself in the shadows, hoping to catch the maiden unawares.

Sometimes, the sun glints off the horn. That's her only warning. Once, it nearly catches her, but it ruins its chances by letting out a frustrated grunt. Without thinking, our maiden drops to her knees, rolling along stones and mud. The unicorn rushes past her, catches its horn in the trunk of a tree.

While it fights to free itself, stamping and screaming, our maiden scrambles to her feet. Crying with exhaustion, she gathers herself and runs once again.

The hunt isn't over.

That's an old motif, by the way. If you can't get a maiden to lure the unicorn, the next best thing is to stand in front of a tree. You goad the thing into charging at you. If you time things right, you can leap clear at the last moment, and let the unicorn drive its horn into the trunk. Then it's a simple matter of stabbing the unicorn to death, or cutting off its horn and running like hell.

Almost sounds like bull-baiting, doesn't it? The unicorn's nostrils flare the same way. Its muscles bulge, eyes go red—they've got tempers. Even Shakespeare said so:

"... *wert thou the unicorn, pride and wrath would confound thee and make thine own self the conquest of thy fury.*"

Timon of Athens. It's no *Hamlet*, but Shakespeare's got to count for something, right?

Pride and wrath. A unicorn denied is a unicorn enraged. This isn't the way the story *goes*, after all. Young maidens should be *delighted* when a unicorn approaches them. They should be *honoured*. They should take the unicorn's attention as proof that they're worth something.

Our maiden is a mess of snot and tears. Sticks and leaves poke from her hair. Her dress has been ripped, and she tugs it lower with a flush of shame. Her other shoe's gone too. She's not going back to get it, but now rocks slice her feet. Every step cuts a little deeper.

And that's just her feet. The maiden's legs ache so much, it's like she's been beaten. She wants to stop, needs to stop. She's too tired to fight any longer.

But she knows what will happen.

Wildness. Pride. Wrath.

The woods are thinning out; she glimpses open fields through the trees. Wide, clear meadows: nowhere for the unicorn to hide. Across the field and down the valley, her village waits. It's nothing much: a handful of thatched-roof cottages that look like gingerbread from a distance.

But the village is home, and home is meant to be safe. Even for quarry.

In the *Hunt of the Unicorn* tapestry, the last panel shows the unicorn tied to a pomegranate tree. The red spots on its flanks aren't blood, but pomegranate juice. Pomegranates are a fertility symbol. Split them open; they look about right.

The funny thing is, they kill the unicorn in the panel before. Then suddenly it's back at the castle, alive and well and dripping with juice. Rather than assuming the weavers didn't know what the hell they were doing, we interpret this as a miraculous resurrection.

But what happens to the maiden?

It never says; we never ask.

Maidens aren't meant to run away from unicorns. Our maiden learns this very quickly. She rushes into her house, slamming the door. Sinking against the wall, she waits for her hands to stop shaking.

She was so scared, in the woods. So very, very scared.

But inevitably, the whispers start. They echo through the market square, run counterpoint to the hymns at church. They follow her to the henhouse, the garden, her best friend's cottage. Wherever she goes, they slide into her ears as insistently as the unicorn's breath.

It's an honour, a privilege.

Close your eyes and get it over with.

Lie back.

It only hurts a little.

Our maiden lies in her cot under the attic's eaves. She cannot sleep. She almost hears the unicorn's dreadful hooves; she tastes its stench and filth on her tongue.

Your daughter's giving herself airs, that's all.

It's unnatural.

Just tell her to relax. It only hurts a little.

But she's not scared of it *hurting*. The maiden twists fistfuls of blanket, the scream bunching in her throat. She doesn't *care* about that. She's fallen out of trees, and cut herself on kitchen knives, and once the cow kicked her. All of that hurt far worse than the unicorn would, she's quite sure.

As with most cottages, there are gaps in the floorboards. Her parents' voices float up from the kitchen below.

At least she's a good girl.

It's past time, though.

Was it something we did?

The same words, over and over.

Unnatural. Wrong. Broken.

The maiden wipes away burning tears. She has not forgotten the blind panic of the chase, the cuts in her feet, or the unicorn's breath on her neck. But at this moment, quivering in her tiny bed, she thinks that being *broken* is worse.

She rolls over, her heart beginning a familiar gallop under her ribs.

She will rejoin the hunt, and this time, she will not run.

Honestly, I'm surprised no one talks about this.

Long, hard appendage. Wild beast that goes after virgins.

But no, no, the unicorn is *itself* a symbol of purity and chastity, even as it places its appendage on virgins' laps. Does no one else wonder about that?

Does no one else wonder: who's really the hunter, here? Is it the man with sword and spear? Or is it the wild beast, stalking the forest for its prey?

Same scene, once again.

The sunlit glade: a cleft in the tangled woods. Grass soft and yielding as a marriage bed. The stream winds between the trees like ribbons through a corset. In the clearing's centre, our maiden sits alone, trying to calm her racing heart. She has a knife tucked under her skirts—for wolves, or bandits. No use dying before the unicorn can get to her. Still, she starts at every sound: the low notes of birdsong, squirrels scrabbling in the branches overhead.

The dread is like metal in her mouth.

It doesn't take long.

The unicorn pushes through the trees. Its nostrils flare. As it approaches, the maiden steadies herself. Remembering the advice—from her mother, her sister, her aunt, her friend—she forces herself to relax. She closes her eyes, because they say that way, it's not as bad.

Coarse hair brushes her arm. Something hard and alien nudges insistently at her thigh.

The maiden grits her teeth. She is not unnatural, she is not wrong, she is not broken. She is quarry and bait together; this is the natural way of things. This is the story she has been told—the story we have all been told.

The stiff horn pushes harder against her. A low moan of pleasure issues from deep within the unicorn's chest. Its tongue flicks over her cheek, and the maiden bites back a sob.

Soon enough, the hunter will come. The pain will end. Her part in the hunt will be over, and she will be maiden no more. Such is the natural way of things; such is the way of the hunt. In all the hunts that have ever been, what maiden ever feared the unicorn?

But our maiden cannot bear the rasp of its goats' beard on her cheek. She chokes on its musk. The horn trails across her skin, edging closer to the juncture of her legs, and disgust rolls low in the pit of her belly. All her life, she's tried to see beauty in the unicorn's mismatched parts. She's listened to the poetry, and looked at the paintings, and she's walked the woods in hope and terror of glimpsing it.

All her life, the maiden has tried to understand. And now, she has finally realized: she doesn't *fear* the unicorn. She's *repulsed* by it.

"No," she croaks. "No, I don't want to."

Even as she says it, the whispers resurge.

Why were you in the woods, then?

You let it into your lap.

It's fine, don't worry. It's just the love it bears fair maidens.

"No!" She shoves the unicorn away. Its ears press flat to its skull, but she's struggling backwards, her fingers grasping uselessly at the grass. "No, I won't!"

She gets her feet under her, stands upright before a tree. The unicorn lowers its head, preparing to charge.

The maiden never kills the unicorn. She always disappears after some male figure appears and does it for her. The usual story in a nutshell: virginity furthering someone else's ends, no matter what the maiden herself thinks.

But we left the usual story a while ago.

Our maiden doesn't like unicorns. That's fine, too.

Not everyone does.

If you can't get a maiden to lure the unicorn, the next best thing is to stand in front of a tree. You goad the thing into charging at you. If you time things right, you can leap clear at the last moment, and let the unicorn drive its horn into the trunk.

We haven't mentioned the hunter yet. There's no strapping woodsman rising to the rescue. In the end, you always face these things alone. And so as the unicorn struggles to free itself, the maiden withdraws her knife.

With every slice into the monster's neck, she cuts away another thread of shame.

Unnatural.

Wrong.

Broken.

No.

Our maiden is quarry, she is bait, and she is hunter. She is the hunt all unto herself, and she needs no one else. It is not the story she has been told, it is not the story of a thousand poems and songs and paintings, but it is *her* story.

At last, the thrusting brute falls quiet and still. The maiden wipes her knife on the grass, tucks it back under her skirts. She leaves the horn where it is: wedged into the wood.

She has no use for it.

The hunt ends as it always does: with quarry, bait, and hunter.

And the maiden, free at last.

K.T. Bryski is a Canadian author and podcaster. Her short fiction has appeared in *Daily Science Fiction*, *Strange Horizons*, and *Apex* (among others), and her audio dramas *Six Stories, Told at Night* and *Coxwood History Fun Park* are available wherever fine podcasts are found. She is currently at work on her next novel. K.T. is a graduate of the Stonecoast MFA in Creative Writing; she also has a mild caffeine addiction. Visit her at www.ktbryski.com.

AUTHOR INTERVIEW WITH K.T. BRYSKI

JASON SIZEMORE

K.T. Bryski is a Canadian author and podcaster. Her short fiction has appeared in *Daily Science Fiction*, *Strange Horizons*, and *Apex*, and her audio dramas *Six Stories, Told at Night* and *Coxwood History Fun Park* are available wherever fine podcasts are found. K.T. is a graduate of the Stonecoast MFA in Creative Writing. I am pleased to bring you an interview further examining her trope subverting story "The Love It Bears Fair Maidens."

Jason Sizemore: In "The Love It Bears Fair Maidens" you subvert the mythological purity of unicorns to great effect. Is there any inspiration you can discuss that gives the story such power?

KT Bryski: "The Love it Bears Fair Maidens" is partly a story about consent, but it's also very much a story about asexuality. The increasing diversity in SFF is wonderful, but there isn't much asexual representation yet. There is some—Karen Healey has written ace characters, for instance—but not much. Most stories still operate on the assumption that consensual, adult sexual relationships—in their various forms—are universally desirable. It's like how we collectively assume that unicorns are pretty and sparkly and everyone wants to see one.

Well, not everyone likes unicorns. I suppose the main inspiration behind "The Love it Bears Fair Maidens" was the desire to show an asexual narrative as equally valid. That self-doubt and assumption of brokenness isn't uncommon, I'm afraid, and I wanted people to understand that, a little. Unicorns just happened to be a really, really apt metaphor.

JS: At no point does the narrator play coy with the story's symbolic phallic representation of the unicorn's horn. For example:

> *Maybe it's black, maybe white, or maybe even gold. It doesn't matter. What matters is that the horn is very long, very thick, and very hard.*

Was it difficult to leverage the forcefulness of this symbolism as emotional fuel against the real possibility of simply being too blunt?

KTB: I was frequently nervous that I'd gone too far. This was definitely a story that scared me, and I did have the urge to tone it down: to rephrase and sidle away…

But I want every story to scare me, in some way. If you're scared, you're writing beyond your comfort zone. And in the end, I had to trust the voice of the story: this bitterly sarcastic, exasperated, crass narrator. When a character (even unseen and unnamed) speaks that strongly, you listen.

JS: There is a lot of talk these days of "safe spaces" referenced in a derogatory manner. But there's a moment in your story where your maiden protagonist has fled home seeking respite from the demands of others, and yet she hears her parents' voices through the floorboards saying:

> *At least she's a good girl.*
> *It's past time, though.*
> *Was it something we did?*

Do you think certain fairytales feed into the misunderstanding of "safe spaces" for people?

KTB: First, let's talk about "safe spaces." Back in my misspent youth, "safe spaces" (or "positive spaces," as they're more frequently labelled up here) simply meant a space where hate speech and/or exclusivity were not tolerated. I think people do still use that working definition, but "safe space" does seem to be taking on connotations of spaces wherein dissension and discomfort are not tolerated.

I do not think that anyone, ever, should be made to feel unsafe. However, there is a difference between feeling

> *This was definitely a story that scared me, and I did have the urge to tone it down: to rephrase and sidle away…*

unsafe and feeling uncomfortable, and I think that's the distinction that's been lost.

Looking to fairy tales, I'm not sure if they feed into this misunderstanding of "safe spaces," but I do observe that when fairy tale heroes and heroines feel comfortable, the story is generally not progressing. Donkeyskin might be relatively safe working in the palace kitchens—but what does she learn, if she stays there forever? Who does she become? What if Bluebeard's wife lived in comfortable ignorance of what lay behind the locked door? What if our maiden never went to face the unicorn?

The deep, dark woods are not a safe space. They are not even a comfortable space. But if you don't brave the trees when you have to, you won't reap the boons on the other side.

JS: When your story was originally published, on Twitter *Apex Magazine* reader Holly Berry (@hollylynwalrath) brought up the issue of trigger warnings. Do you feel that trigger warnings add a stigma to a story?

KTB: No, I don't. As Holly wisely said, the reader has a right to know what they're getting into, particularly if it's a context in which one might not expect disturbing content. I actually gave myself a trigger warning earlier this year, for one of the episodes in my podcasted audio drama Six Stories, Told at Night. I could see how the content might be upsetting, and so a warning seemed appropriate. To my mind, effective trigger warnings function like the rating systems for video games and movies—a courteous heads-up about the content therein.

That said, while the reader has the right to know if a story contains potentially disturbing material, they also have a responsibility to manage their reaction to it. It's like allergies, in some respects: I'm allergic to wasps, so while I don't demand the obliteration of every nest, I'm very careful when I know they're around.

In sum: appropriately-deployed trigger warnings are courtesies, not condemnations.

THE GENTLEMAN OF CHAOS

A. MERC RUSTAD

People call him the Gentleman of Chaos, but he is not gentle.

By popular count, he's assassinated thirteen kings, seventy-two princes, one thousand nobles, and five queens.

By popular legend, he's immortal, a god of commoners, a death-demon summoned to feed on corruption, a shadow that devours the unjust. He never unmakes the innocent, it is said.

He is not gentle; I have seen what he does.

But I tell you this: part of his title is true. He is a man. And men can die.

My brother the king was cautious. He took the throne when he was twelve, the night after our father was murdered. With the crown not yet heavy on his head, he called me to his private chamber.

My brother said, "I need your help, sister."

I was six. I said nothing.

He nodded, grim-faced, and sent me away.

Three days later, when I was locked inside the Abbey of Mercy, I heard that I had been declared dead; a tragic drowning accident. My funeral was spectacular, I am told.

The Gentleman of Chaos has been painted, illegally, in a thousand different ways: as a winged shadow descending like a hawk against the moon; as a tall, thin wraith cloaked in starlight; as a man with knives for hands and eyes like an owl. He wears armor, or he is naked. He dances across rooftops or rises from the cobbled streets like mist. He smiles or he is faceless.

Always, somewhere in the paintings or the stories, there is blood. Blood on his fingers or in his mouth; blood dripping from his clothing or falling around him like salted rain. Blood that pools for a thousand miles beneath his heels.

He has no name, for it was banished long ago. By royal decree he has no face, for he does not exist. No one has heard his voice, soft like velvet; no one has seen the exhaustion and pain in his eyes; no one has felt his hand, scarred and calloused, on their cheek in an apologetic caress.

No one has heard him whisper, "Not yet, child. Not tonight."

Because he knew how our father died, my brother laid his plans in delicate layers over slow years. I did not see him again in person until I was twelve, when he visited once to ensure I was what he had commanded I become, but I always knew his voice, his words, his will. It wrapped around me like iron cords. Not a day had passed in six years that I did not know my brother's wishes.

My brother shaped me, built me into the perfect bodyguard — skilled in lies and unable to lie to him; deadly in the arts of poison and steel; loyal only to him; unremarkable in looks but my body trained until I had exacting control over every muscle, every breath. I had no title and no name. My brother called me She.

I was forged with one purpose: to serve my brother, to protect his body and soul, so that he might reign long.

The Gentleman of Chaos has no past. Or perhaps those in power wronged him, had his lover murdered, imprisoned his child, broke and re-shaped his body, strove to take away his will and identity.

It doesn't really matter, because he doesn't exist.

"I dreamed ill omens last night, sire," I told my brother.

The king clutched his goblet until his knuckles paled. "What omens?"

"The Gentleman of Chaos is coming for you."

He scoffed. "With you, She, I am always safe. Isn't that true?"

"Yes, sire," I said. I did not lie.

My brother the king married twice, yet both wives died in childbirth, their stillborn infants strangled with bloody umbilical cords. Courtly tongues spun rumors of sorcery, a curse carried in the king's seed.

"Did you do this, She?" he asked me, tears glistening in his eyes.

I told him no.

"Then how?" he screamed. "Who did this?"

"The Gentleman of Chaos," I said.

The king did not remarry.

On the day I was released from the Abbey of Mercy, my brother the king summoned me to his side. He held a slim iron collar engraved with old magics.

"It cost a fortune to have this made by the reclusive wizards to the north," my brother said, "and even more to have them killed afterwards. But it will be worth any price. This is yours, She."

I held motionless as he snapped the collar about my throat.

"She," he said, "will obey all orders from my lips. She will never harm me or let me come to harm. She will never lie to me. She will serve until death."

The collar was unbreakable, permanent.

I did not let the king see my hatred; it was private, mine alone. Though tempted, I did not ask him, *If you had a brother, would you be as merciful?*

I simply bowed and said, "What do you command, sire?"

At sixteen, my brother gave me an ultimatum: by my eighteenth birthday I must have given birth to a healthy child. He did not care who I bedded. I was to have my pick of any man not of noble breeding, and as many of them as I liked.

Not a tiresome order as I enjoyed the company of men. I fucked a dozen of them, experimenting in what I liked, what I didn't. They were tools, just as I, and I used them as such. I never learned their names; they were guardsmen or bakers or stable keeps or scribes.

At seventeen, I was pregnant.

The first public attempt on my brother's life came during the autumn ball when I was eighteen. The Count of Dunfly, an unambitious cousin twice removed, hosted the masquerade. My brother had crushed the Redgrove

Rebellion in the spring, prevented the Ishzaven from uprising on the northern border with carefully executed genocide the winter before, and eradicated the Musavo from within the kingdom that summer.

A very successful legacy in so short a time, said the court, a reign worthy of celebration. He would continue to do great things, his advisors told him. He made examples of commoners who dared to insult him and call him the Bloody Prince. ("I am king!" he told me as we watched the executioners make public spectacle with screams and gore.)

My brother the king was invincible so long as She was there to guard him.

As my brother danced with the Countess of Dunfly, a woman twice his age, I drifted in the shadows of gaudy gowns and pleated suits, gilded masks and lacy-scoured hats. As always, I wore black: trousers and a tight-fit vest that flattened my chest; no loose threads or stray fabric that might be used against me.

I smelled the sweet rot of lilac before I saw the assassin, dressed in a beautiful lavender suit and carrying a fan sewn from dyed swan feathers. I threaded between the dancers and caught the assassin by the wrist before the fan, tipped in needles, could brush against my brother's skin.

"Dance with me," I whispered, and spun the assassin away.

"You will never protect him," the assassin said between clenched teeth. "You will fail one day."

"No," I said. "I never fail."

Fifteen steps later, at the end of the waltz, the assassin slumped in my arms, the fan's needles embedded between his fingers. I let him fall like a drunk beside a marble pillar and continued to watch my brother.

I knew what the baby was. Leverage, a thing to hold over me.

My brother the king, who thought he had a sister, was not so arrogant that he did not fear me. I was with him always. I shadowed him when he went hunting, when he held court, when he danced, when he fucked whores and married duchesses alike.

I could not become soft, so I did not nurse the baby. She was given to a wet woman and I could only visit her once a month, under guard, in my brother's presence. He watched me, all but unblinking, as I stood with arms folded at my back, staring down at the thing I had pushed from my womb.

She looked like me, the baby did: she had my eyes,

brown and wide, and my nose (but not broken yet). Her complexion was lighter, like the man who had fathered her. I thought, one day, she might grow up and smile.

I did not ask what name my brother had given her.

The Gentleman of Chaos is not cruel.

He is a sadist. He tortures his victims and rips out their souls.

He kills them painlessly, quickly, and they never know they are dead.

He says rites over the corpses; he curses them before life flees their eyes.

He wears the trophy-teeth of his victims and he leaves a black-dyed rose with each.

No one has ever conversed with him and lived to speak of it.

"There's too much inconsistency!" my brother spat. "How can he be a sadist and also show mercy? You're lying to me, She."

I pointed at the collar. "She can't, sire."

He paced in his bedchamber, empty tonight of female companionship. I sat like a bird of prey, a great vulture, on the leather ottoman at the foot of the bed.

"Then tell me how all these stories can be true!"

"All stories contain truth, sire," I said. "One must be willing to see it."

The guardsman's name was Vyren. He was stationed in the outer city, keeping nebulous order in the streets in the aftermath of the unsuccessful coup against my brother's throne.

I asked him if he wanted a child with me. My brother, after all, did not care who fathered my offspring. When Vyren agreed, understanding it would be some years before he could know who the child was, I fucked him for weeks until I knew the seed caught and I conceived.

Vyren was a good man. He wrote me notes and left them where only I might find them. He cared for his younger brothers and his elderly mother with his wages as a guard. He smiled, for he still knew what happiness was — warm food, sleep, laughter with others, sex, watching the rising sun, defending his family from injustice.

"What if I told you I don't see myself as a woman?" I asked him one night, as we lay together in the dusty hallway, away from spying eyes and wagging tongues.

He propped his head up, elbow crooked, and looked down at me. "I'd tell you I like you just as well."

"You wouldn't be lying?"

"No," he said, and kissed me. "I like *you*, Vessai. Man, woman, something else — it doesn't make me feel different. I like all of you."

Something in my chest cracked, like glass beneath a booted heel. Not a physical rending of muscle or bone, but as painful, as vivid.

"I fear I love you," I whispered. He laughed, but I couldn't join him. "I've never loved anyone since … my parents."

"Not even Free?" He used our daughter's name with care, for that was what he thought we should call her, no matter what the king decreed.

"I don't know how to love her yet," I said.

Vyren pulled me closer to his chest, his sweat and mine mixed into pungent musk. He stroked my shaved head; hair was a liability and a vanity. "One day, Vessai, things will change. I don't know how or when, but they will. We'll see our daughter again."

I shut my eyes, a luxury I did so seldom. His heart beat steady and sure against my ear. "I need you to do me a great favor," I said.

The Gentleman of Chaos visited me in the Abbey of Mercy when I was ten. He stood in the high, narrow window, a silhouette of death against the moonlight that lit the chapel vestibule.

I knelt inside the granite penitence circle, my wrists chafed bloody by ropes, my back aching from the Mother Superior's cane. I had not been fast enough; the cloth and clay mannequin representing my brother had been stabbed before I could put myself in the knife's path.

"What do you need?" asked the Gentleman of Chaos.

"Nothing," I said. "I need nothing."

"Be careful with that word," said the Gentleman of Chaos. "It holds more than you imagine."

I glared at him.

He drifted down from the window, with rope or silent, unseen wings, and prowled toward me. I saw no weapons; I saw only death.

"No," he said, and sat cross-legged at the edge of the penitence circle, a band of iron inlaid in the floor, with razors set against springs that would snap at the slightest pressure. With one finger, one smooth caress against the iron, and I would die, pierced by a thousand razors. "It is not your time, Vessai."

That was my *name*. Not the one bestowed at birth, but the one I called myself.

I gritted my teeth. "Why not?" I was the only one in my family save for my brother. My mother, so my brother wrote, had died of grief after I left. The weight of two lives bore into me heavier than the Mother Superior's cane.

"You are nothing yet," he said. He reached out, his hand long, but only his shadow touched my cheek. "Be patient, child."

Then he stood and vanished again through the window. "He comes closer every year," I told my brother. "I feel him. I hear whispers from the vultures and the ravens."

"Hunt him down," my brother said. His voice cracked in tension.

"I would," I said, "but She cannot leave your side, sire. I will be ready, however, when he arrives."

He stared at me, his teeth grinding.

In the end, he did not send me away.

My brother the king was not a kind man.

The guardsman and I stood before my brother in a small, private study left to spiders and dust on royal decree. It was where my father had been killed so many years before, where I had once played under the table with toy soldiers and horses.

"You've consorted with an assassin," my brother said.

"Sire," the guardsman said, still at attention, "I would never —"

"She." My brother gestured at me. "She is an assassin."

The guardsman swallowed and glanced at me sidelong. I remained motionless. When I'd spoken with him, roughening my voice, meeting his eye as men do, he'd never known my brother called me She. It was an odd-fitting word, one that chafed like the collar.

"Do you know what assassins do? They target royalty. They target *me*." My brother paced. "You've slept with her. You gave her a daughter. You would turn her against me."

The guardsman backed away. I'd already taken his sword when we entered the study. "No, Sire, I've never —"

"Kill him," the king told me.

I slit the guardsman's throat and lowered his body, half-shielding his face from my brother's sight. His blood spurted over my tunic and I tasted salt. His gaze never left me, even as he choked.

"I'm sorry," I murmured in his ear, and it was not a lie. He had died in Vyren's stead; a man who looked similar, one with whom I'd let myself be seen around so my brother would suspect.

I was a vulture, circling the dead.

When I was twenty-one, my daughter asked to see me. Ever benevolent, my brother allowed me a visitation. He watched us from the balcony as we sat on the garden bench by the fountain.

"Do I have a father?" the girl asked.

I watched her, emotionless. "Everyone does."

"Yes, but who is *mine*?"

I did not respond. She had inherited my shrewdness; she would know if I led her astray.

"The king says he's my father," the girl said quietly. "But he's lying."

"Do you know who your mother is?" I asked her.

She shook her head. "He says she died when I was born."

We stared into the fountain. Our eyes were so alike.

"Maybe she did," I said. "But if a king is your father, that makes you heir to the throne, doesn't it?"

"I guess," my daughter said.

"And that means one day you will be queen."

She kicked her heels against the fountain's rim. "Could I be a good queen?"

"Yes, child, you can."

The Gentleman of Chaos lives in nothingness. The dark of the moon is his bed, the twilight his dawn. He appears to the wicked in their time of destruction.

By popular account, he never fails when he chooses a target.

Popular legend is a lie.

"Sire," I said to my brother as we ate in private. He had taken a fancy to the old study; I had left several tiny bloodstains from the guardsman's murder on the stone. "It's time we acted."

"No one gives me orders!" He grabbed my throat. I watched him, unmoved, and waited until he loosened his hold, leaving the imprint of the collar pressed into my skin. "I am king. I! I decide when it's time!"

He sat back, breathing hard. His eyes were bloodshot. He had not slept well in weeks, haunted by nightmares. Every sound startled him; every footstep made him twitch. I tasted his chamomile tea each night before bed, and never had it been poisoned; he did not understand why he could not rest without waking in a sweat, screaming.

The nightmares were delicate beasts, carved from lace and feathers, bright teeth dripping and cold. They paraded the faces of the dead before his eyes, skeletons wearing the masks of murdered innocents.

"Your word is law." I tilted my head. "What does the law command?"

He threw his plate across the room. The shattered glass made him flinch. "I want the Chaos man dead. Do you hear me, She? Dead. In torment, damned forever! See it done!"

"Of course, sire."

When he retired to his bedchamber, I tasted his tea, let the dreambane wash off my tongue into the warm chamomile, and gave him the cup.

I sat in the steam bath adjacent to my brother and considered my body. Hardened, scarred, shaped with binding leather straps and cloth to give it a more masculine profile. I was indifferent to my breasts; they would never nurse, and I had no sensation in my nipples from the hardening agents injected into sensitive flesh by the Sisters. It was only on my brother's orders that they had not sewn shut my cunt, because he wanted me to bear a child one day.

Every time I sought out men to fuck, for enjoyment, for *myself*, I pictured the Mother Superior's face and laughed. The Sisters made competent assassins out of girls who were deemed undesirable.

I never admitted to the Mother Superior that she had been tricked into training a man.

At fourteen, on the eve before I was released from the Abbey of Mercy, the Gentleman of Chaos returned to me.

He slipped through the window, a shadow against the dark I lived in, and I leapt upon him. I laid a blade against his throat as he did mine.

"Is it time?" I whispered. "For our deaths?"

"That is your choice."

Temptation ached inside my chest. "Why didn't you kill my brother from the beginning? You could have spared me all this."

His eyes were filled with sorrow. "When I calculated the cost, I could not. If he died that night, so would you. Your mother would have her throne usurped. There have been jackals in the courts for years, ones your father barely kept in check. The king has eliminated them now. But then? War would have overrun the land. I hoped that if you lived, one day, you would take the throne and restore balance."

"All this?" I hissed, leaning closer. His knife broke the skin of my throat and I did not care if it cut to bone. "For a hope?"

"I have made worse mistakes," he said softly. "And so will you."

He lowered his arm. I did not.

"You could have saved him!" My hand shook. "You could have saved my father."

"We all fail," said the Gentleman of Chaos. "You know your brother the king; you know what he will do."

"Then end him," I said. "Fix your failures."

"I am dying, Vessai. I have been for years, since you came here. I ask you to take my name, become the next Gentleman of Chaos, as I did once, as the one before me did so long ago."

"Why?"

"Because now," he said, "you are nothing."

He caught my wrist and guided my hand. I slit his throat and let him fall. His blood was no different than mine, spread along the stone floor.

It was the only time, since my father's death, that I cried.

"Sire," I told the king, "my ravens whisper that the Gentleman of Chaos is here."

His bloodshot eyes were wild. "Tell me where!"

"He will come to the palace chapel, below where your father died. He will come alone."

"I will have an army waiting, then!" cried the king.

"Sire," I said, "I have lured him here with the rumor that on the full moon, you pray alone and will be unguarded. If he sees soldiers, he will disappear again and haunt you longer. Allow me to finish this."

The king stared hard at me, his jaw working. "It will end?"

"Yes," I said, and it was not a lie.

The Gentleman of Chaos glided from the shadow, through moonlight patches that danced from the stained glass windows in the palace chapel.

My brother knelt in a show of prayer, unarmored, unarmed, exposed, trembling as his ragged breath filled the chapel.

"She?" the king called. "Protect me!"

She was gone. She had been fading for years, piece by piece, eaten away by time and realization that She had never been a woman.

There was only the Gentleman of Chaos.

The night my father was murdered, I was hiding under the heavy table, my toys clutched in tiny hands. Blood spread under the tablecloth and stained my feet.

I'd watched my brother stab our father again and again after Father told him, quietly, in private, that he would not be named heir.

"You have no heart, my son," Father had said with great sadness. "A king cannot rule without heart."

"Lies," my brother had shouted.

Neither of them had known I was under that table, because I was always a quiet child.

"I hear your grief," the Gentleman of Chaos murmured, his hand drying my tears.

"Can you save Father?" I asked.

His eyes held all the sadness in the world. "I'm sorry. I can't."

I grabbed his hand and held on so he would not vanish and leave me alone. "Then will you kill my brother?"

"Not yet, child. Not tonight." He kissed my forehead and whispered a promise, "But I will show you how."

The king looked at me, wide-eyed, gasping without breath. I, the Gentleman of Chaos, carefully set the king's heart in his own hands.

Impossible, formed on the king's lips. His heart dripped and stilled in his fingers.

The Gentleman of Chaos unclasped the useless collar that had controlled She. It had never bound Vessai — it had bound a lie, and I had lain that lie to rest at last. I was not She. I was not the sister of the king. I was Vessai, and now the Gentleman of Chaos.

"Magic only binds the true self," I told the king.

I would see my daughter on the throne, for the king had named her heir. She would always be safe, with Vyren at her side to guide her, and the Gentleman of Chaos would always be her shadow.

I would spread my vulture wings and I would haunt the world, as my predecessor had, and all those who had come before him.

The Gentleman of Chaos is not a gentle man.

His hands are red, his eyes are dark, and his heart is heavy.

He serves a just queen from shadow, and no assassin will touch her. She will bring balance; she will rule well. This loyalty, this service, the Gentleman of Chaos shows his queen is born from love.

He will never again let a king bind him.

A. Merc Rustad is a queer transmasculine non-binary writer who lives in the Midwest United States. Favorite things include: robots, dinosaurs, monsters, and tea. Their stories have appeared or are forthcoming in *Lightspeed, Fireside Fiction, Apex, Escape Pod, Shimmer, Cicada, The Best American Science Fiction and Fantasy 2015,* and *Wilde Stories 2016.* Merc likes to play video games, watch movies, read comics, and wear awesome hats. You can find Merc on Twitter @Merc_Rustad or their website: http://amercrustad.com.

LAZARUS AND THE AMAZING KID PHOENIX

JENNIFER GIESBRECHT

The first thing the Old Man told me was this: "Sometimes folks just don't die right."

So I'm gonna tell you a story about what that that means, and I want you to listen real carefully.

The Old Man said to me: "Sometimes they go down. Sometimes they go down, down, right down to the bottom. Right to the center of it all, but they don't stay there. They come right back up. That's what you done, son. You came right back up." He told me this with his cold, dusty gloves cupping either side of my face. He had to hold me down so I didn't keep screaming or else I might have done that until I died the right way.

My skin was still charred when I first woke up. I raised my hands above my head and watched as it bubbled and leaked, as it grew pink — then brown — between the charcoal scabs. By nightfall I was covered in an armor of abscess. I spent six hours popping yellowed sacks of pus to reveal my new skin, baby-soft and unmarked.

"What do you remember?" the Old Man asked me when I could speak. My tongue was still numb from blistering, my eyes hazy and cheeks raw from where the skin had sloughed off in rubbery sheets. I didn't remember, I tried to say. It wasn't true — I saw glimpses of it in short, painful bursts. Tiny, knife-shaped headaches that ground through my skull like diamond. I remembered some ugly words and the grate of a lighter being clicked to life over and over again. I remembered tripping over my shoelaces and hearing a song somewhere in the distance, a hard grind of sax and bass. Funk was a false promise of kindness. *Will it go 'round in circles?* Billy Preston was asking me. *Will it fly high like a bird up in the sky?*

"I burned," I told him. "They freaking burned me. I died burning."

"A lot of things die burning," Old Man Gasper said. "But not you."

Before I burned, I fancied that I could have been a comic book writer. What Dad wanted for me was to go to Berkeley, like he did, and we argued so fiercely about it that it was the last thing we talked about before he went and got himself crushed on the highway by an eighteen-wheeler on the way home from a lecture. I figured at least writing comic books I'd be safe; locked inside a dusty one-room apartment eating beans out of a can.

What I liked about comics was that they only had so many pages, right? Tolstoy could write as much as he damn well wanted to tell us about *War and Peace*, but Stan Lee only has twenty-four pages to show us how Spider-Man learned about responsibility. When I was a kid, comics could only use four colors. That's why Dad thought they were juvenile. He used to criticize them for being emotionally shallow, for not being able to capture anything but the broadest expression of human experience. I was too young to articulate it when he died, but what I'd tell him now is that full expression is not the point. When you can only use four colors, you choose them carefully. Distill them down to their purest and most immutable form.

That's the argument I still have in my head with my father — that comics express the Platonic ideal of emotion. At least, that's how I understood things at the time.

LAZARUS AND THE AMAZING KID PHOENIX, ISSUE #1

PAGE 1

Panel 1:

Text Box: THE CURIOUS ORIGIN OF THE AMAZING KID PHOENIX. A BOY THAT CAN BURN WITH THE HEAT OF HADES! WATCH HIM LEARN, WATCH HIM BURN, WATCH HIM BURN DOWN THE WHOLE ENTIRE WORLD.

Panel 2: (Picture this: Chicago, 1972. It's a dark alley on a stormy night. You know the place, man, it's every alley in every city all over the US of A. There's trash cans and rats with slavering mouths and giant, cartoon-red eyes. An owl hoots somewhere in the distance, a premonition. Real spooky stuff.)

Panel 3: (A kid barrels down the narrow between buildings. 5'7", skinny and knobby at the joints. About 16 years old, African-American and growing into a handsome man if you believe what his mom says (and his mom doesn't lie). The kid's not terrified. He's running with purpose, because he's being followed by villains and he's gotta lure them into a false sense of security.)

Panel 4: (He (heroically) skids to a stop. Sound effect: SKEEEET. He wheels around — not panting, not out of breath. He's grinning because he's got something in store for *them*.)

Panel 5: (Who are *they*? Three shadows block the entrance of the alleyway. The second half of the panel is eaten by a gaping, plump mouth. There's an angry gap between its front teeth, an abyss of ill intent, darker than the night.)

Panel 6: (Light spills in from the streetlamps. Our villains, illuminated: a pack of dumb looking thugs wearing matching red jackets and high-collar shirts. One has a narrow rat face, the leader is pig-nosed. He's a clear contrast to our hero, who is clean-cut and comely with large eyes and a trustworthy smile.)

THUG: We're gonna teach you a lesson, nerd! To show you what happens when you stand in our way!

(The leader of the pack flips out his butterfly knife and snarls.)

Panel 7: (Our hero puts his hands on his hips and stands proud. He is the single bright point in a dark, corrupt world.)

KID PHOENIX: And I'll teach you what happens to lowlifes who try to deal drugs in my neighborhood!

Panel 8: (And aren't they *surprised* when our Hero bursts into flames.)

Old Man Gasper was a hulking figure packed all uneven and lumpy into a canvas suit that didn't hang right on his body. It folded backwards around the joints and bunched up over the rims of his boots and gloves. He wore a gas mask and a mining helmet and he never took them off. He left no part of himself visible to the outside world. In the evening, he sat on a milk crate and talked to me about philosophy, his harmonica grasped loosely in the open crib of his hands. We stayed in a bare room with no electricity. The dying light turned all the shadows on his body into fathomless canyons.

On the sixth day he told me — in that molasses Appalachian accent of his — about his troubles: "When I was just a bit older than you, I used to work in the mines. A lot of things go wrong down there. Already halfway to hell is what my pa used to say."

His voice evoked the image of shadows moving bent-backed through the fog. Of mist rolling down the green mountain in soft folds. Gasper sighed: "They don't care none about what happens to a coal miner in the depths. A coal miner ain't nobody but a coal miner's son. When I burnt up, they just closed off the tunnel."

I tried to imagine it: the steam bursting up around him like a living thing. A beast made of translucent fang and smoke claw. Its silk tendrils slide beneath his flesh. It makes his veins snap and pop, makes the skin roil with greasy, white bubbles. The image shivered through me.

"When my body dissolved in the steam no one came back to check," he said. "I laid in the ink like one of the horrors what lives on the bottom of the ocean and never ever dreams that the sun might exist. When I crawled back into my suit, I didn't even noticed I'd changed."

It took time for me to noticed I'd changed too. On the sixth day, I looked just fine, but my bones felt like they were trying to jump out of my skin. I traced lines over my face, looking for imperfections. I'd pinch at my neck, my knees, the inseams of my elbows, any place where the skin hung loose and soft. I felt like I was something new underneath and maybe I could peel away my flesh like a sheet of cellophane.

I was scared that I really was dead and I'd turn gray and smelly like the zombies in Romero's films. That was probably why the Old Man wouldn't take off his mask, I decided, 'cause he smelled like pig's ass.

It took a week before I stubbed a bare toe on brick and got so mad that I burst into flame. Blew the windows right out of the abandoned apartment we were staying in and stained all the walls with soot-shadows. Ashy firebirds with jagged, angry wings.

Old Man Gasper wasn't even upset. He just took off one of his big, leather gloves and showed me how there was nothing underneath but tendrils of pale, smoky film. He had no hands. He had no *body*. Gasper hadn't just died in the steam, he'd *become* it.

"When it first happened to me I had this fear that God didn't want me," Gasper said calmly. "Then I thought about it even more and got afeared that the Devil didn't want me neither. I couldn't figure out what I'd done in this life to make both the Devil and the Lord too mad to look me in the eyes."

He took off his mask to show me that it was hollow as well.

"Well, yeah, sure they don't want to look in your eyes," I joked. "I mean, man, come on — you don't even have eyes anymore."

He laughed and an involuntary shudder rocked right through me; the man I was talking to, he had no mouth, no throat, no body to make that noise. His shape was only human because something in the steam remembered what it was like to be shaped like a human. It was as close to having a conversation with a man's soul as anyone ever got.

Gasper leaned forward — the elbows of the empty jacket settling on rubber knees in a motion that was driven by pure force of nostalgia. "The flames gave you another life, son. I'm going to show you what we do with it.

LAZARUS AND THE AMAZING KID PHOENIX,

ISSUE #3
PAGE 1

Panel 1: (Our heroes stand on a roof, vigilant. The night sky is dark, but their silhouettes are made bright by the light of a dollar-coin moon.)

Text Box: LAZARUS AND HIS AMAZING SIDEKICK, KID PHOENIX, HIT THE MEAN CHICAGO STREETS TO BUST UP ITS MOST NEFARIOUS CRIMINALS AND GANGBANGERS!

Panel 2: (Lazarus is chasing down a thief. You know that it's a thief 'cause he's clutching a purse to his chest like it's a baby. Lazarus's arms extend as smoke from the confines of his suit. His hands look like fluffy clouds as they wrap around the thief's ankle.)

LAZARUS: Halt!

Panel 3: (The thief has toppled over! He crumples against a brick wall with his tongue lolling out of a dog-like mouth.)

Panel 4: (Lazarus — ever the kindly and soft old man — holds the purse up triumphantly. His gas mask is twisted in a big ol' grin.)

LAZARUS: Tsk, tsk, tsk. Didn't you know: *pearls before swine* is just a turn of phrase!

(Kid Phoenix arrives on the scene, his eyes glittering with red fire.)

KID PHOENIX: Golly gee, Lazarus. I guess he better stick to ham sandwiches from now on!

Panel 5: (Lazarus claps his kid sidekick on the shoulder, like a proud father.)

LAZARUS: He'll get all the ham he can

eat at the state penitentiary!

The Old Man only had a few possessions. He had a set of encyclopedias, 1968 edition. He had a harmonica and he grew plants. He said that he liked plants because the Egyptians used a germinating seed to represent the rebirth of Osiris. I didn't even know what Osiris was. I was more interested in his fourth hobby, which was sitting on a roof at dusk and looking for trouble.

"You only take a crime within five city blocks of where we're staying, and never one out in the open." He told me the rules, counting them on his fingers one by one. "Never one where you'll be spotted, or one that you think the police will attend to. And you don't take one where the criminals are kids, or they look wretched."

"This is so cool," I said. "It's like we're Batman and Robin."

The Old Man stared at me, silent, vapor curling quizzically in the eyes of his mask.

"You gotta be kidding me, you've never heard of Batman." I snorted. "Of course, you were born in what, 1750?"

"1882," Gasper corrected.

"So, if you've never read *Batman*, why do you do this?"

The Old Man was quiet a moment. "I didn't at first," he said.

"What made you start?"

"I met a lady, one like us, only she were worse done by it."

"How do you get worse done by than burnt to death?"

Gasper set his palm on my head. "Well, son, her husband beat her so bad that when he was done with her she looked like a sack of meat with no shape."

I could feel him trembling through the glove. My imagination, I guessed, because the Old Man didn't have the flesh or the muscles or the nervous system to quake from any emotion at all. It was probably me who was shaking.

"He dumped her in a quarry afterward and she laid there a week in the Arizona sun. Then she came back up and looked at her reflection in the water. You want to know what she told me she saw?"

I leaned forward and propped my elbows up on the lip of the building. It didn't hurt anymore to grind my skin between brick and bone. "A lady with her head caved in?"

Gasper shook his head.

"No, because my lady friend, her head didn't stay caved. Where she got hit, she grew a new bone where there wasn't bone before. That's what she looked like — six joints in her arm, armour made of teeth coverin' her face. She was magnificent. She said to me: 'God wants you.' She said: 'God wants us more n' ever.' She believed that so sure that she gored six men to death in just the first month after she came back up. What she saw in the water, she said, was an angel."

"What happened to her."

Gasper said nothing.

I was filling up inside, welling with a strange anxiety like the sky was getting bigger all around me but I just kept shrinking until I was too small to even comprehend the stars. I asked: "Did you see her again, then?"

"No." Gasper answered.

"So, what? We do it 'cause God wants us to? Like your lady friend said?"

"Son," the Old Man said solemnly, "God doesn't exist. But we do, and so did she. Now, watch carefully."

What Old Man Gasper did was that he creeped right into a man's throat and held onto it gently. The man we got, he'd cornered a woman like a wolf corners prey, like a sheepdog herds ewes. He had her flat against the brick with a snarl and something clenched between his fingers that glittered in the streetlight.

The Old Man said to me: "Shhh," and he seeped from the gaps in his coat, from the muzzle of his mask. He snaked through the night air, a quivering ribbon of silver, leaving his boots and coat and shroud deflated in a pile at my side. The man breathed him in without even knowing it. The Old Man became a hitch in his throat and the criminal pawed desperately at the skin of his neck as heat poured down his esophagus.

Old Man Gasper asphyxiated the man slowly, gently. Carefully. Filled his throat and his nose and his lungs just long enough to interrupt respiration. The man folded in on himself, crumpled right in front of his victim, limbs all crooked.

"She never knew a thing happened," I whispered when the Old Man got back. She pulled her jacket tight around her and fled. I looked at my own hands, turned the flame on and watched the dirt burn off, felt strangely cool inside the cage of immolation. The fever burning in my chest was a comfort, the spark between my teeth a power.

"I couldn't do that," I said. "I couldn't do it so that no one knew a thing happened."

"We'll figure it out," the Old Man said. He was confident. He always sounded confident, probably since he was nearly a century old.

I spent the next week on the roofs, watching. The Old Man had a system, but he was *so* cautious. He was cautious in a way that made my bones rattle and my nerves go taut all around my joints. Gasper did small deeds, saved small people. I had fingers that could turn into tendrils of heat, a heart that was newly molten at its core.

"I could just burn the whole thing down," I told him one night.

"What would be the point?"

"The whole wicked place. I could find the fuckers that burned me and I could burn all their shit down, Old Timer. I could do it."

"And would that bring your mother peace?"

I went to my place sometimes, got up on the fire escape and pressed my hands to the window, trying to catch of glance of Mom and my brothers. I always played it safe. Never stayed long enough to see a smile or a sob. To see if Mom's hands were shaking. It was too soon, I knew, too soon after Dad for me to have died too. The Old Man said I could go back if I wanted, but it was impossible. I'd been all the way down, right down to the bottom. You can't look your mother in the eye after you've seen the bottom of the world.

What was I supposed to say to her? "Oh hi Mom. Just so you know, the world is a vast, dark and Godless place. It's brutal and violent and I just want to set fire to the foundations. I want to dive beneath the Earth's crust and shake up the magma until it pops through the pores of the planet and we all burn together." That's how it felt. I was scared that if I looked her in the eye, that's what I would have said.

"Sorry, Ma'," I'd say to her, my hands turned to flame. "I guess I'm a monster now."

Instead I began to read the encyclopedias. I'd set two beside me and read them front to back in a day. I'd never known I could read so fast before I had a literal flame burning at my back.

"Lazarus," I said, my finger on the name. "Lazarus and Kid Phoenix."

"Hmm?" the Old Man wheezed between broken harmonica notes.

"They're our names, Old Timer. You spent three days dead in a cave and I was born in the flame."

"Lazarus spent four days dead, son. I don't get where you're going with this metaphor."

"It's not a metaphor, it's our Hero Names."

"Like Batman and Robin?" he asked.

I snapped the book shut and laughed. "Only better.

Batman ain't got powers, man."

But I could, you know. I could do it easily. I could burn everything. That's what I thought.

And why shouldn't I have? It hurt, sometimes, to bottle it. To feign ignorance. It put a crack in me. It put a crack in everything.

LAZARUS AND THE AMAZING KID PHOENIX, ISSUE #24

PAGE 7

Panel 1: (The body tumbles through the rough underbrush. She's wearing a powder blue dress, dappled gently in polka dot and ruffle. It holds the shape of her doughy body. It is loyal to the memory of her curves and dips.)

Panel 2: (The murderous husband walks away. In his shadow, we see her hand resting lifeless in the yellow grass. It is puffy, puckered purple with thick, dark bruises. One of her fingernails is missing, the others bent and splintered. Her nail polish is still immaculate.)

Panel 3: (She lays beneath the sun and it bakes her rotting flesh. Flies find a home in her nostrils. She goes down, all the way down, right to the bottom —)

PAGE 9

Panel 4: (— she looks in the water. The wind makes ripples that obscure her features. At first, the reader will think that the reflection is a lie, that she has awoken whole, that a good woman like her will be given a second chance.)

Panel 5: (The water stills. The sun burns behind her and the anger burns inside her. She no longer lives inside soft, mortal skin. She lives inside a cage of bone, a suit of armor. She is reborn a warrior.)

PAGE 20

Panel 1: (When she smiles, her teeth grind together. But she *does* smile.)

HER: Gasper, you are a sweet man, but you're milk soft.

Panel 2: (Gasper's lady friend has a vicious mouth. Her blue eyes are buried inside a skull that's overflowed through the skin. Her face is a mask of teeth. Rows and rows of them, tumbling over each other as they splinter from the trauma of growing too close together. There are molar roots peeking through the fray; tiny, white devil horns to pierce the skin of any man stupid enough to hit her again.)

HER: God wants you. God wants us more than ever.

Panel 3: (She fans out her hands. They have too many fingers. Try to count them: seven, nine, twelve, too many. Enough, she once told Gasper. Enough for her new purpose.)

HER: What does Isaiah say about the Seraphim, Mister Gasper?

Panel 4: (Her fingers become wings. The teeth along her cheekbone sprout feathers inlaid with a thousand eyes.)

HER: He said that they were horrors, and that they hurt him to look at.

Panel 5: (Inside her eyes burns a wheel of fire. I'm watching in a dream. I look at my hands — at the fire that webs between my fingers — and I shudder.)

HER: He said that they were born in flame.

Panel 6: (She stands on a hill and watches the sun set. The Old Man describes her like this: that despite the horror and the bloat of her body, she was still beautiful. There is a purity about her, as if she is haloed by the blood she's spilled. A polka-dot dress sways around her elephant knees. She spreads her arms and lets the Lord's light shine down on her. The horizon ignites.)

HER: I am a Horror, Mister Gasper. I am an avenging angel.

Gasper and I ran down cutpurses, but we stole hot dogs. When I asked him why, he said: "I don't believe in money. When I was a boy, we didn't pay for food. We ate our own chickens. It's sick to make a man pay for food."

"I wouldn't have taken you for a Marxist." I laughed, because my dad was a Marxist too. Whenever he got raving, my mom rolled up the newspaper and whapped him on the back of the head. She told him to be practical because: *Wouldn't it be nice to own a dishwasher someday, Marshall?*

"I never thought about it that way before. I just don't think it's right."

"Hey — you were alive when Marx was alive, weren't you?"

"Only for a year. Don't think that counts. Besides," Gasper chuckled cryptically, " 'The past is a foreign country'."

"Still, it's wild. Give me a high five, man."

"Kid, I ain't got no hands, remember?"

We spent a cozy six months like that. It was glorious, let me tell you, the way I would ring the street in these teeny, tiny fires, like the kind you think you're so bold for setting with toy pistol caps. I set fire to their shoes. Once, I got naughty and ruined some carjacker's leather coat. Only the cuffs, though. Wouldn't have wanted to get *extreme* or anything.

The Old Man was kind with me, but he muzzled my potential. He put a cap over my steam engine and the pressure, it just built and built and —

"— are you listening?"

I grit my teeth and dug my nose deep into my comic. I was getting an earful about the jacket. "I bet Batman never lectures Robin like this." I turned the page noisily.

The Old Man's expressions were pretty easy to read: the whole suit shifted from one side to the other when he was pleased. Smoke flickered in his goggles when he was concerned. I sometimes wondered what he'd been like as a whole person. Craggy and toothless and southern, I figured. He hadn't been educated until after he died. It gave him a strange manner: a hillbilly mouth with a post-Civil Rights demeanor. He pitched forward and snatched the comic book from my hands. Who did he think he was? My *dad*?

Yeah, right. My dad never let me read comic books. He'd have me reading Plato or Descartes or something. *You have to work harder than your friends*, he always told me. He never said why out loud, even though we both knew. We just weren't that kind of household.

Gasper began flipping through the comic. "I don't think I like Batman very much."

"*Dude*," I grabbed it back. "Who doesn't like Batman? He's right up your alley, Old Man. Doesn't kill the crooks, not even the really bad ones."

"He's got too much money," Gasper said. "I don't trust men with money." He paused, then added: "Robin don't look much like you either."

Did he really have to point it out like I didn't see it everywhere I looked? "Yeah, well. That's why when I grow up, I'm gonna write comics." I folded the pages open and touched the soft newsprint. "I'll write one for you, Mister Gasper: hillbilly Batman and black Robin. Would that make you happy?"

Gasper didn't reply.

"Or maybe we can go collect your lady friend. Recruit a new guy who died in a glue accident or something. Make our very own Fantastic Four. Our very own happy family of *freaks*."

"Hmm," is all he said. He sat down on his milk crate and retreated inside the suit. I couldn't tell what the fuck he was on about. I hopped up and stretched out my knobby limbs. I paced the length of the warehouse and fumed.

There was a feeling I had, a thing that needed doing. Something I had to do or my bones were going to char themselves into ash.

LAZARUS AND THE AMAZING KID PHOENIX, ISSUE #4

PAGE 1

Panel 1: (A bank robbery in progress! The Kid Phoenix arrives and assures the bank tellers that he has the situation under control!)

KID PHOENIX: Have no fear, Kid Phoenix is here! I'll stop those dastardly crooks using the oldest of all man's superpowers ... the power of FIRE!

Panel 2: (The robbers are already inside the vault, stuffing their greedy suitcases with cash! The head crook is dressed in a gray, pinstripe suit with a blue ascot — the very image of capitalist scum.)

Text Box: THINKING FAST, THE KID PHOENIX FORMULATES A PLAN!

Panel 3: (Kid Phoenix slams the vault door shut and presses his burning hands to the metal.)

Text Box: USING THE POWER OF CONVECTION, THE KID PHOENIX BEGINS TO HEAT THE VAULT LIKE AN OVEN!

(The metal begins to turn red under his hands. His palms breathe heat.)

KID PHOENIX: Sorry folks, but it's about the get awfully hot in there! If I were you, I'd surrender!

Panel 4: (Inside the vault, the criminals are sweating. The walls are red and pulsing, but the worst they'll suffer is the effects of an overzealous sauna. Kid Phoenix's flames merely tickle. It's not like he could actually *kill* anyone!)

Text Box: THANKS TO THE KID PHOENIX'S AMAZING INGENUITY, THE CROOKS ARE GIVEN LITTLE CHOICE… WHAT INCREDIBLE FEAT WILL HE ACCOMPLISH NEXT!

PAGE 2

Panel 1: (The Kid Phoenix reunites with Lazarus on a rooftop. They bump fists in solidarity, a symbol of their partnership.)

LAZARUS: Where to next, chum?

Panel 2: (Kid Phoenix has one foot on the lip of the roof. He looks like a very noble gargoyle, awash in the colors of the sun.)

KID PHOENIX: Wherever there are women crying and babies who need their candy back! We'll go —

Panel 3: (Something catches his attention. His eyes flicker dark. They go bottomless.)

(What he sees: a boy leaning a girl against the wall, laughing into her mouth. They share a joint, passing it back and forth as they snicker at some private joke. The colour and light drains out of the world. Why were you drawing this as if it were midday, you dumb-ass? Something like this could only happen at night. Kid Phoenix and Lazarus are monsters who hide during the day.)

Panel 4: (The boy is blond and fresh-faced. His lips pucker thick and pink beneath a light dusting of orange freckles. He's cute, the girls say. He wears his hair in feathers, like Robert Plant. His hand nudges under the girl's skirt and traces the curve of her buttocks. She throws her head back and giggles. They're happy. Just two kids messing around under a streetlamp.)

KID PHOENIX: … motherfucker.

PAGE 3

Panel 1: (Kid Phoenix makes fists and digs his nails right into the skin. He draws them along the shallow ridges etched into his palm from a short, uneventful life. *Just two kids messing around under a streetlamp, not a care in the fucking world.* No one passing by would guess that one of them is a goddamned murderer.)

Panel 2: (And so the Kid Phoenix begins to move. He dashes for the fire escape. He's gonna burn the fucker until he's just a stain on the wall.)

(Lazarus grabs him by the arm. Jerks him back, turns him around so they're staring at each other in the black of the night)

LAZARUS: *Don't.*

Panel 3:

(Kid Phoenix is breathless with anger, confusion and fear. *How dare you deny him this!?*)

KID PHOENIX: I have to.

(Lazarus doesn't let him go. He holds him so tight that steam crawls out between the seams in his gloves. He doesn't understand. He wasn't murdered, not like Kid Phoenix. Not like his old Lady Friend. Gasper died alone in the dark. No one meant for him to die. Kid Phoenix spits.)

KID PHOENIX: Fuck you, Old Man. *I have to.*

Panel 4: (Lazarus lets him go and holds out his hand.)

LAZARUS: Promise me you won't.

Panel 5: (Like all children, Kid Phoenix knows that the only way he can be free is by lying. Like a dog chewing off its own leg to escape a trap, the Kid Phoenix lies, he lies, he *lies*. The lies burn beneath his skin, white as a supernova.)

KID PHOENIX: If that's what you want, Old Timer.

I stalked my murderer down the way he'd stalked me.

No, that's not right. He yanked me out of a burger joint by the scruff of my jacket. When I stalked him, I did it *methodically*. I learned his habits and his hangouts. I learned the best time to find him alone.

"You're not still thinking about it, are you?" the Old Man asked me. He asked me three times over two weeks and each time I smiled at him, white teeth all a glimmer. I looked so honest in my mind's eye. I really thought I had fooled him.

The night I planned to do it I swept into our warehouse, a sulfur tornado of fury and purpose. I grabbed my jacket and a lighter. I grabbed my book bag and stuffed it full of comics and encyclopedias because I guessed that the Old Man would never let me come home after what I was planning to do. His suit — slumped in the corner where I'd left it — came to life as I zipped the bag up.

He said my name and I snapped, straight backed, to attention.

"Don't go back out," he said firmly. I bit my lip to stop myself from saying something I'd regret. Then I un-bit and said it anyway.

"You're not my keeper, Old Man. Mind your own fucking business."

He rose a limb at a time. The pieces of his suit didn't always move in concert with each other, especially not when he was upset.

"I'm telling you now, son, that you should really reconsider your course of action."

I let the bag fall from my hands. I let it fall because my palms had turned to flame and angry as I was, I really didn't want to burn the Old Man's copy of Encyclopedia Britannica Vol. XXII. My breath caught hard in my throat as I pieced it together: he'd followed me. The flames climbed up my arms, swirled under my armpits, crawled out from the shell of my ear and whispered against my temple.

"You trying to tell me what to do, Old Man?" I ground out slowly. "You wanna tell me what I can and can't do with my anger?"

Gasper was so calm that it made my eyeballs pop from the heat. "I just want you to stop. Just for a breath, now, son, and I want you to think."

"I *am* thinking, motherfucker!"

"No, you're *feeling*."

"Yeah, feeling kind of *betrayed*. You were spying on me! You don't *trust me*."

"It ain't like that."

"Then what is like!?" I shouted. My tongue was a curl of red lead. I burst open the seams of my own body. The fire tore through me, crumbled my skeleton and dissolved my flesh in a moment of white hot blistering revelation. I unfolded like a lotus. Seared the encyclopedias, peeled out the windows and engulfed the warehouse we lived in inside a cocoon of flame before collapsing in on myself like a dwarf star, recomposing my shape from muscle memory. I gasped greedily, sucked all the oxygen I could and rekindled the heat that was eating my heart alive. I'd never felt so *fucking alive*.

Gasper took a step forward and seeped through the seams of his suit. "Son," he said softly, "Kid, you …"

"Always 'Son' this, 'Kid' that," I hissed. "Call me *boy*, you fucker. Come the fuck on. I know you want to."

Gasper held up his hand and cocked his head towards me, as if I should hold up mine as well. I did so, begrudgingly, because I was the kind of kid who always listened to adults. Then I saw what he saw: my left index finger no longer existed. It was simply gone, replaced by just the thinnest haze of heat. I stared at it dumbly.

The Old Man unhooked his coat. He unspooled the thick, rotten leather in one heavy click and let the front fall open. The inside was the colour of rust, or dried blood. The atrium of his coat was not empty.

There was something at the center of him, suspended by the steam and pulsing gently in the scorched air. A tangle of capillary veins, a spiderwebbing of tense, quivering nerve clusters. All that was left of Old Man Gasper.

"It doesn't last forever," he said. "Don't know that I'd be trying to keep you here so desperately if it did."

I shook my head, numb with denial, still staring at my own hand.

"We all wake up whole, son. And we all wake up angry."

I went anyway.

LAZARUS AND THE AMAZING KID PHOENIX, ISSUE #1

(SECOND DRAFT)

PAGE 1

Panel 1: (We paint a romantic picture because it plays well with kids. A more accurate drawing dilutes the focus, it confuses the narrative. This alley is a different kind of dirty. A garbage bag has split open, spilling coffee grinds, rotten hamburger, cigarettes, a used needle. Our hero is on the ground, his wrists bound with a telephone wire.)

Panel 2: (The boy with the lighter kicks him twice in the gut. Calls him a word that the guys down at the Comics Code Authority aren't gonna approve no matter how many asterisks you put after that 'N'.)

BOY WITH THE LIGHTER: Fucking *punk*. Man, what made you think you could deal in our neighborhood?"

(He didn't. He didn't think that at all. Our hero wasn't even dealing, kids, you have to believe him. Yeah, he sold a few grams to a friend of a friend because… fuck, who knows why he did it? Isn't everyone doing that shit these days? Because he'll never be 6'1" like his dad was? Because his marks are good enough to do what his parents want him to do, but he wanted to try something different. He wants to be cool. *What the fuck even is "cool"?* He just turned seventeen a week ago.)

Panel 3: (One of the gang grounds the hero's face into the cement with his boot.)

THUG: Was it worth it, cocksucker?

HERO (ME): L-look, this is a mi-mis-understanding. I —

Panel 4: (They begin dousing him in kerosene. Oh god, oh god. They won't really do it. Some of these kids are middle class, they have reputations to save. *They're just trying to scare me, they wouldn't really —*)

ME: P-please, my M-mom's expecting me home. She'll … she'll call the police

if I'm late. I —

PAGE 2

Panel 1: (~~My~~ The hero's mouth fills with gas. That shuts him up. *If I were white, they'd just have some fun kicking me until my teeth came out. Like, they'd beat me so I walked funny. I could deal with that.* The hero opens his mouth to beg them to beat him, but the gas is in his lungs. He coughs and spits.)

Panel 2: (The leader flicks his lighter on. The grind of the flint is like a clap of thunder. CLICK, CLACK, CLICK. He is all shadows. Only the white of his eyes and his gap-toothed grin are lit by the flame.)

THE BOY WITH THE LIGHTER: *Boom.*

Panel 3: (*He lights me up and I scream and I scream and I go down, all the way to the bottom.*)

I tucked myself in a dark corner and waited, arms crossed and my thumb held up in the universal symbol for 'good luck'. I flicked the tip of it on and off like a lighter and tried not to think about what was missing from my other hand. I was already coiled up bright and mad when he rounded the corner.

"Hey man," I sauntered out of my monster's hidey-hole, feeling fifteen feet tall, "remember me?"

He didn't. Not immediately. He had to squint and look me up and down twice.

"Are you fucking kidding me!?" The rage stung the pads of my fingers and steamed out through my pores. "How many black kids have you iced that you can't even remember the *face of someone you burned to death*?"

Recognition clicked into place and his features lined up to make the perfect picture of panic. He licked his lips dry in the rising heat and readjusted the collar of his pressed, salmon shirt. All he could say was: "Oh."

Yeah, I could taste his fear. It wasn't sweet. It was kind of dull, not even bitter. My anger was a better flavor: molten metal, searing my tongue with the sting of a thousand and one spices. I began to glow like a piece of heated copper. My veins turned neon carmine beneath my skin.

He — my murderer — took a step back. My flames licked at the heels of his boots. Soon, they'd be licking at his face. Licking down the walls of his esophagus. I'd dive down his throat and crumble him to ash from the inside out like a demented lover's kiss. I'd curdle him like milk.

And then I'd keep going. I'd spread my Phoenix Wings until they embraced the entire fucking city. I knew that I could. I felt it inside of me, quiet and self-assured, a radioactive core of bright and terrible possibility. I was gonna burn him down, and then I'd burn the city, the state, the whole goddamn world. Burn and burn and burn until I stopped, until I couldn't burn anymore. Until there was nothing left.

My murderer opened his mouth to scream, to plea, to beg, to call me that fucking word again. I waited, a single, bright boiling point at the center of the world, simmering patiently as I waited for him to waste his last breath. Waited and waited.

All that came out was an aching, rattling howl. Two thin ribbons of steam came crawling out from his nostrils. His eyes rolled back and he fell over, dead. Suffocated from the inside out.

I was so incandescent with rage that it took me a minute to realize what the old man had done. He hadn't listened to me. He'd stolen my revenge. He'd saved my life. He'd *killed a kid*.

I toed the boy over and watched the last bit of steam roll out from his mouth. It dissipated in the evening air, used up. Gone forever. "You stubborn asshole," I whispered. "I *told* you not to follow me around."

Old Man Gasper did not answer.

LAZARUS AND THE AMAZING KID PHOENIX, ISSUE #25

PAGE 24

Panel 1: (Our hero stumbles out into the street, dazed and drunk off emotion. He sees the familiar suit, crumpled in a lifeless heap in the middle of the road. He falls to his knees and pats it down, desperate. There is nothing inside.)

Panel 2: (It's empty for real this time. It will be empty until the end of time.)

KID PHOENIX: It doesn't last forever.

Panel 3: (The Kid Phoenix lifts Lazarus's mask and holds it up to the light. He looks at it for a long time before laying it back down in the street. He leaves it there as a memorial, all that is left of Old Man Gasper.)

I wish I could tell you that I never killed anyone, but that just isn't true. It's the furthest thing from truth I could tell you.

I mean, I'm not even certain that's what the Old Man was trying to tell me. So yeah, I burned a few people in my time. But I learned that fire has other uses.

You know that the only reason we have civilization is because of fire, right? Fire is the reason we don't fear the night, and it's the reason we can live wherever we want. Fire is used to build every single piece of a watch. The immutable form of heat is not destruction, it's creation. It's a creature that can hold you with both hands.

I don't know why I came back. It doesn't matter if I tell the story in four colors, or in four hundred, I always arrive at the same place.

And that's where you come in.

LAZARUS AND THE AMAZING KID PHOENIX, ISSUE #??

THE LAST PAGE

The Last Panel: (You, a tiny ragged girl with a knife-chopped haircut. When I saw you first, you were huddled beneath the black skeleton of your home. Your parents were pillars of ash. You are small and angry.)

YOU: You want me to act like nothing ever happened?

ME: No. But you should know it won't last forever.

YOU: You never explained why we come

back.

ME: That's because I don't think it matters.

YOU: He died for you. Are you trying to be like him? It won't change anything.

ME: I know that. I've kept you warm because I want to.

(You are warming your hands over a dying fire. The flame sputters, chokes into
embers. My voice is soft now.)

ME: Fire has so many uses.

(You lean in close. The fire is a whisper.)

ME: It can be used to keep a single person warm, down here at the bottom.
Until they come back up.

(The embers cool. There is nothing left of them. They are cold and gone forever. You hold your hands in front of you and shiver as a salty, winter wind
washes through you. This is the last time you will ever be cold. You take a
deep breath and gather your courage.)

(You come back up.)

Jennifer Giesbrecht is a native of Halifax, Nova Scotia where she earned her degree in History and Methodol-
ogy. She's a freelance editor, multi-disciplinary nerd, and a graduate of Clarion West's 2013 class. Her work has
previously appeared in *Nightmare Magazine*, *XIII: 'Stories of Resurrection'*, and *Imaginarium 3*.

CUCKOO GIRLS

DOUGLAS F. WARRICK

"You never wait to see if it's really dead," says Samantha, leaning over the small arsenal configured in pristine rows on the linoleum. "Because, you know, it isn't. You just put it down for however long, and you run. You try to make it to a new place before it gets back up." Her voice is casual, conversational, friendly. She might as well be discussing a particularly esoteric hobby, trying to recruit new participants, but not trying too hard. She picks up one of the Molotov cocktails and sniffs the rag. "What, did you soak this in gasoline?"

"Well, yeah," says Nikki. "I mean, was I not supposed to?"

Samantha shrugs. "I mean, whatever, it'll be fine, probably." She sets the Molotov down on the kitchen floor and starts reconstructing her field-stripped Kahr CM9, her fingers juggling the components of the handgun with precise and practiced thoughtlessness. "I've always soaked the rag in alcohol or kerosene. Filled the bottle with gasoline. Come to think, I'm not sure why I've always done it like that. Read it on the internet, probably."

A sense of anxious uselessness blooms up from Nikki's guts and spreads in her chest. Watching Samantha do this stuff, watching her slam together pieces of little death machines and listening to her expound on best practices when building homemade incendiaries, seeing the shiny burn scars that peek out from beneath the collar of her shirt, trophies of the times she has survived, it all makes Nikki feel like a child. This isn't her kitchen. It's not anybody's kitchen. It's a tiny kitchenette in an extended-stay hotel, another place that doesn't belong to her. How long is she supposed to live like this?

"Now, what the pros do—I mean, not pros, exactly, but serious revolutionaries, you know—they fill the bottle with… shit, I can't remember. Anyway, they fill the bottle with one kind of chemical and wrap the bottle in paper soaked with another kind. Can't remember the chemicals now—ugh—so dumb. When the bottle breaks, the chemical in the bottle reacts with the chemical on the paper, and boom." She sets the CM9 aside, picks up her sports bottle of lemonade and takes a long drink. Offers it to Nikki. Nikki wants it. She's been parched all evening. But she says no. Some part of her doesn't want Samantha to give her anything. Some part of her is afraid of what happens to people when they become Samantha's friends.

Samantha's already back at it, picking up weapons, checking them for whatever it is people who know weapons look for, setting them back down. "Oh, and if you mix the gasoline with egg whites, it'll stick to concrete and burn longer. That's a cool idea, I think. Really solves a problem I wouldn't even have thought about. I love stuff like that."

Nikki says, "We're not throwing them at concrete."

"Well," says Samantha, "we're not revolutionaries, either. And, um, my advice? Find things you like to talk about. Learn how to talk about them without stopping. It helps."

Nikki doesn't say anything.

It doesn't happen to everyone. Not that many people even know about it. Most people who deal with it walk around their whole lives thinking they're the only one. Sometimes, they die before they ever get a chance to form complex opinions. Sometimes, they survive for decades and never meet anyone else like them. But sometimes, they run into a thread on a message board or discover a lonely hearts ad in the back of a local weekly constructed with just the right level of esoteric specificity to mean absolutely nothing to anyone who doesn't know what it's like. Sometimes, someone else just recognizes the dark hollows around their eyes and the way they keep glancing at all the exits.

That was what it was like with Samantha and Nikki. There was this bar, this super high-class place where dudes wore suits and ordered clear drinks and discussed stupid boring shit in practiced newscaster tones. Nikki didn't notice at the time just how out of place Samantha seemed in there, with her plaid shirt and the paisley bandana barricading her short hair off her forehead. Remembering it, that's all she can think about. How conspicuous she looked.

She'd almost forgotten her name at that point. Weeks after the thing had done what it had done to her friends and family, weeks of driving, of whittling away at her meager savings, of trying and failing to sleep, of showing up in new cities and wandering aimlessly, putting herself in places filled with happy functional people in the hopes that their pristine fearlessness would inoculate her from what had happened ever happening again.

She'd sat down at a corner booth and pulled Brett's North Face jacket close to her face, tried to inhale whatever was left of his scent. It just smelled like sweat and gas station food. Every time glasses clinked or one of the coiffed suits laughed a little too loud, she cringed and whimpered.

And then Samantha was sitting next to her, sliding into the booth with expert gentleness, placing a bottle of beer in front of her. "Hey," she said.

"Um," Nikki said. "Hey."

"Got you a drink," said Samantha.

"Oh. Thank you."

"You just look like you could use one."

Nikki picked up the beer absently. Muscle memory. For a while, Samantha just sat there, nodding in time to the opulent blare of brass instruments in whatever Rat Pack tune was playing through the sound system. Glancing at Nikki, appraising her. Then, she said, "What'd yours look like?"

It took Nikki longer than it should have to process the meaning of those words. When she did, some ragged hybrid of terror and hope gripped her by the ribcage and she made eye contact with Samantha.

Samantha nodded, offered a sympathetic half-smile. *I know. You're not the only one. It's okay.*

"Skin like… I dunno, like beef jerky." The tears. The panic hitching in her lungs, fucking with her breathing. "Tall. There were, um… always lightning bugs. Fireflies. Wore a… like, a mask."

"They usually do," said Samantha.

The Glock 19 scares Nikki. It feels so unbearably natural in her hands, a statement of purpose, a promise. She thinks of all the things she knows about guns now that she didn't know before. The ergonomics of the grip,

the debates within the firearm enthusiast community between autoloader advocates and revolver fans, recoil and the ways to minimize it, Weaver stance, isosceles stance, blah blah blah. She thinks about her stance, tries not to think about the pinch and ache of the protective earmuffs. She tries to keep her muscles loose, fails.

Firing ranges don't look like they do on cop shows. They're brightly lit and busy. Undramatic. But her target—a white sheet, a vague implied man-shape—is just about the same. It feels strange to be aiming at something with mundane human dimensions and trying to imagine it as the thing from which she's running. Like training to become a surgeon by applying Band-Aids to papercuts.

She fires six shots, hits a button, watches the white sheet proceed down its ceiling track toward her. She pulls off the earmuffs.

Samantha leans against the wall of Nikki's booth and scrolls over something on her phone. "This girl on one of the message boards," says Samantha. "She thinks they're some sort of gods. Listen to this: 'Something is controlling them. Someone. They're being summoned, they have to be. And we're the fuel that keeps them in this dimension. Without our blood and our fear, they can't manifest.' How do you like that, Nikki? Purty spooky."

Nikki examines the holes in the target. "God, I suck," she says.

"Doesn't make sense to me," says Samantha. "They're so fucking clumsy. It's not, um… I don't know… not clinical enough to be ritualistic."

Three shots over the left shoulder, passing cleanly through fuck-all. One in the left shoulder. Two in the left arm. Nothing to the chest or head.

Samantha speaks again, ostensibly to Nikki but apparently to her phone. "I met this woman a couple years ago who had worked out this big elaborate theory that we were film characters. Like, each from a different franchise or property or whatever. That the reason they don't ever stay down is because somebody keeps writing sequels. I like that one. It's so fucking meta. I mean, whatever, who knows if it's true, but you gotta admire that kind of abstract reasoning."

Nikki is only half listening. It's always like this. Nikki constantly tense and anxious, constantly waiting for everything to go to shit again, and Samantha scouring every available source for something to fill the silence with. Her voice has become a weird comfort, the third member of their partnership. When they sleep, Nikki always tries to drift off first. If she doesn't, she won't sleep all night. The silence feels like a sucking void.

"I don't like that one," she says. "I don't like, um… being diminished like that. All this for someone else's entertainment."

Samantha shrugs. "It's only a theory," she says.

Most girls who survive, they're usually the only ones. That's how you know it's there for you and not for your friends. The pattern is always the same the first time it comes. It saves you for last. Lets you escape a few times. Plays with you, satisfying itself with whomever you've surrounded yourself with in the meantime. Your parents. Your friends. Your boyfriend. And then it starts hunting you in earnest. The process sometimes lasts weeks, but typically plays out over the course of a single evening. According to the message boards, there have been a lot of incidents that seem like they fit the usual pattern in which the target dies with the rest of them, and they're the subject of heated debate. Who was the target? Why didn't she survive like we did? Is this really one of ours, or is it unrelated? Can we learn anything from it?

Truth is, you can't learn anything. Ever. There aren't any answers.

Nikki never stops smelling it. Manure, wet asphalt, baby powder, bonfire smoke, the ripe sweetness of garbage long past needing to be taken out. That scent has haunted her since the moment it loomed over her in the unfinished basement of her parents' house, its smiling baby-doll mask so close to her face that she could see that it wasn't a mask at all, could see the way it pulsed and rippled as alien musculature clenched and unclenched beneath it. She forgot about the fireplace poker in her hands. The stink overpowered the smell of Brett's blood, which was all over her and had been all she'd been able to smell for hours. In retrospect, that seemed like a reprieve. In a lot of ways, she'd rather be haunted by the ghost of that thing's scent than by the ghost of Brett's last scent. She wants to remember the way he smelled before. Cigarettes and a little too much cologne. The way his jacket smelled before she ruined it with fear sweat.

Down in the basement, it strained its overlong neck closer to her, cocked its head to one side, like it didn't quite understand her, like it was personally wounded by her refusal to die. A single firefly crawled out of one of its eyeholes, floated in the tiny space between them, glowed once, then flew away. Nine feet tall, all of its limbs absurdly long, hunched like a very old man to keep from scraping its head against ceiling beams, clutching her father's big straight razor like an ape that happened upon a tool it didn't understand. Her father had loved that razor. Kept it sharp. Took good care of it. Inherited it from mom's dad when he passed.

She was all out of tears. All out of screams. Empty except for a panicked understanding that her life had winnowed down to a stark binary: she would either die tonight or another night. That's all there was. All there ever would be. When it raised the absurd disproportionate fist that clutched the razor, she stabbed it in the belly with the fireplace poker. From the wound flew hundreds of fireflies.

The stable is on fire, the thing that hunts Samantha is on fire, and Nikki can't stop looking at the flames, twitching, swelling, thrashing. The heat evaporates her tears before they can slide down her cheeks. At the fire's core, the thing slumps to its knees, stops waving its thickly muscled arms above its head, falls over sideways, is still. Samantha's monster at the climax of her latest sequel. Nikki does not look at the burning thing. She does not breathe. There is only the fire, slowly making its way up the wooden beams, consuming this evening's hiding spot, consuming Nikki's awareness, filling her with numb disgust. She did this. This was her.

Then Samantha's got her by the arm, dragging her away, past the stalls, out of the stable, into the cold night. The thoroughbreds shriek and thrash in their stalls. Nikki, ever haunted by sensations, still hears the sound of the bottle shattering. Still feels the sudden rush of heat from the Molotov igniting. She is here and there. Now and then. Stuck in two instances overlaid into simultaneity.

They bee-line for the fence, ducking down and crawling through the hole Samantha cut to gain access to the stables this afternoon. There had been one more of them, then. A third girl. Esther, whom Samantha had found on the message boards. She'd been nearby. Frightened and confused and alone. They had picked her up, promised to keep her safe. They were broke, but Esther thought that if they could get into the stables, they'd have a place to crash for free. Sleep among the horses and figure out the rest tomorrow. The thing that killed her wasn't even hers. Samantha's did it. Surviving doesn't make you a survivor. You die tonight or you die another night.

They get to Samantha's car, buckle their seatbelts, slam the doors, turn on the fucking radio, and they can still hear the horses screaming as they burn to death.

Samantha drives.

"I killed it," says Nikki. The words escape her like air from a balloon. "I killed it."

"No, you didn't," says Samantha.

"I burnt it. I killed it. It killed Esther, and I killed it."

"No. Nikki, you need to stop."

"But I did it, I beat it, I beat your monster, I—I—I… did it. It was me."

"Nikki," says Samantha, "hon, I need you to shut up right now, okay? Just shut up and let me drive, okay?"

"But, Samantha, I—"

"Nikki!" Samantha shouts. Nikki has never heard her shout.

She shrinks back involuntarily. "Shut the fuck up. Now."

They get on the highway. Drive without talking. It's the first time since they met that Samantha has been silent. There's a baseball game on the radio, and Nikki thinks of Brett and tries not to cry.

They stop for gas twice, depleting their already dangerously low funds. Samantha has been at this for a while, has had to make money before now, surely. Between panicked non-thoughts and flashbacks, Nikki wonders how.

The sun is starting to come up when Nikki sees Esther's purse in the footwell. She picks it up, opens it, extracts her wallet. Fifty bucks. A debit card. Two credit cards.

"I had this theory," says Samantha. Her voice cracks. She's been crying. This whole drive, Samantha has been crying without making a sound. "I thought… fuck… I thought maybe the things that are after us couldn't touch a girl that didn't, uh…" she swallows, "align with them… like, I thought since you were hunted and I was hunted, the thing hunting me couldn't hurt you. The thing hunting you couldn't hurt me. Fuck, Nikki. I was wrong. Jesus."

Nikki doesn't say anything. She thinks about reaching over and putting her hand on Samantha's knee, but her limbs tingle bloodlessly, and she's not sure she can move.

Samantha pounds on the steering wheel with the flats of her hands. The tears come conspicuously now. The wall crumbles, and Samantha, scared and angry and tired of everything, is laid out in front of Nikki like a dissected frog. "You want to know what I think? Where I really think they come from? No bullshit, no meta-movie stuff or god stuff or stupid message board stuff? I think they come from us. I think it's our fault. We… make them, somehow. They grow in our brains, and then they just sort of… hatch. Like maybe we're not

even real people, like maybe we're just designed to look like people so that nobody notices one of those things growing in their own house. They're cuckoo birds, and we're their eggs, and all the fucked up shit we do or have done to us just bubbles out and turns into them. And they will come, and they'll come, and they'll come and come and come, and eventually, we'll be stupid or tired or sad or weak or… or brave enough to let them kill us. Matter of time, Nikki."

She's silent for a long time. Then she laughs and says, "Prove me wrong."

"It's going to be okay," says Nikki in a voice smaller and higher than the one she thinks of as hers.

Samantha smiles sadly. This is where Nikki realizes that something has changed. That this isn't a temporary break, that Samantha isn't okay. That probably nothing is or ever will be anything close to okay again, if indeed it ever was. "Nikki, you're probably… no, you *are* the best friend I've ever had. I trust you, and I like you, and I love you, and I'm loyal to you. But… and I… *hate*… myself for this, but… if it comes down to you or me? I will let you die."

She reaches over and turns off the radio. The car is filled with road sounds. The sun climbs a little higher. Then she adds, "I won't even think about it."

They always look different. Short and slender, tall and stocky, roughly humanoid, totally abstract. There's a woman on the message boards who says hers looks a little like one of those animatronic animals at kiddy birthday restaurants. Another one says hers looks like a cloud of phosphorescent gas that occasionally coalesces into the shape of a person. Samantha's is short and fat, exuding a slimy film all over its cave-fish pale skin, sexless, naked except for a burlap sack over its head, and its fingers are all fused together. She says it smells like her father. They almost always appear to wear masks.

Some women say that they never saw it coming. That their lives as they knew them ended like someone flipping a light switch, normal one moment and shattered the next. That's not how it was for Nikki.

The first time she saw it, she was sitting on the porch swing rigged up in front of her parents' house. Carrie was over. They were drinking coffee and watching the sun go down, bundled under blankets and winter coats, reliving high school slumber parties past and knowing they were staring down a sort of precipice. Their teenage selves were sliding further and further into history, and even then, hanging out with Carrie felt like putting on a favorite shirt that had grown a little too small. Things were changing. It was sad, but sort of promising, too, an implication of the women they were respectively becoming. Mousy, chubby Carrie was neither of those things anymore, had a boyfriend now, couldn't stop talking about him. Nikki couldn't stop talking about Brett, was equal parts terrified and elated that her parents had invited him to spend Christmas with them.

It was actually Carrie who saw it first. She did that thing people do when something weird hooks their attention, straightening her spine, craning her neck.

"What?" said Nikki.

"Nothing. This dude."

"Wow. You forgot about David pretty quick."

"Shut up."

"You get hot and suddenly you're on the hunt."

"No, shut up, it's not like that. Just… seriously, look at this dude."

Nikki tried to follow Carrie's eyes, saw nothing. "What dude?" she said. "I don't see a dude."

"Fucking… right there. Get your eyes checked. Whatever, it's nothing. He's just… he looked a little weird to me."

Then Nikki saw it. It was… it had to be a man. Two blocks down, where the road curved away toward the high school. Almost, but not quite, standing in the cone cast by the streetlight. He hadn't seemed suspicious. For all they knew, he could have been waiting on a ride or looking for something he'd dropped in the dark. A pang of shame pulsed in Nikki's belly and she looked away. Just a weird-looking man minding his own business being scrutinized by a couple of shitty judgmental college girls. Poor guy.

"He's tall," she said. "Jesus, he's really tall."

"I know, right?" said Carrie. "What's with his neck?"

"I dunno. Some people just have long necks, I guess."

"God. I guess. Hey, look!"

In the front yard, swelling and subsiding to a rhythm they couldn't hear, a tiny green glow. There, and then not there. There, and then not there.

"Aw," said Nikki. "Firefly!"

"We always called them lightning bugs," said Carrie. "Weird. Super late in the season for it."

"It's nice," said Nikki. "They pack the backyard in the spring. Makes this place feel like home."

The nights are impossible now that Samantha doesn't talk as much. Nikki averages three hours of sleep per night. Some nights, she stays awake until sunlight creeps past the blinds of their motel room and sleeps only when her body forces her to do so. She sat up one night and begged, in tears, for Samantha to talk to her, employing the same phrase again and again, wishing she could think of synonyms or speak in a different language or do anything at all to break through the perception she'd developed of her own voice as some sort of terrible broken child's toy. And when Samantha said, "I'm sleeping," Nikki knew she meant, "I'm dying." Sometimes, when she's floating between consciousness and unconsciousness, she thinks she feels Samantha stroke her hair, but she can't be sure if that's real or just a nice dream.

They've been here for two weeks. The motel room looks like a crime scene waiting to happen. Nikki sometimes imagines evidence tags tied to the trigger guards of the handguns on the bathroom counter, imagines gloved hands stacking up copies of *The Anarchist's Cookbook* and old issues of *Guns & Ammo*. She wonders what state they'll be in, what configuration their opened and emptied bodies will comprise, what the detectives and the CSUs will think of them when they open the door and find them torn to pieces. And she knows it doesn't matter. They aren't going to stay. Soon, they'll pack up all this shit and get back on the road. They'll run Esther's credit card dry and they'll dump it in a garbage can and they'll just keep going. This is their life. Run, hide, wait, fight, run, hide, wait. Endless iterations. It almost never bothers her anymore.

Until one night, while Samantha sleeps in the bed next to hers, Nikki sees something glow green and disappear. The blood in her veins turns into liquid nitrogen and freezes her. And with a certainty beyond fear, she knows.

She shakes Samantha, who sits up without protest, looks at Nikki straight on and says, "Do we need to go?"

Nikki nods. She wants to be the strong one for Samantha, wants to reverse roles and put to work everything she's learned, to grab Samantha by the arm and lead her through the motel's third-floor hallway toward the metal stairwell and down to the pool, past it, into the parking lot, away. She wants to give that to Samantha, a gift for all the times she kept Nikki safe and sane. But she's scared, and all the strength Samantha instilled in her has drained away. That long-limbed thing with the fake face. It's here. Somewhere close. Close enough that thinking is analogous to wasting time. Close enough that each heartbeat represents a moment she should have spent running. So she nods, whimpers when she should speak, tries not to cry.

Samantha's out of bed, packing up the guns and explosives, throwing her jacket on, slipping her arms into the straps of her backpack, saying, "We need to be gone six seconds ago. Let's move. Come on. Go."

Nikki obeys. Readies her pack. Straps on the shoulder holster Samantha gave her, checks the clip in the G19, tucks it beneath her armpit, covers it with her jacket. Brett's jacket. But not really. Not anymore. It smells like smoke and dirt from the stables, like cordite, like someone else's blood. For a second, Brett's face rises up in Nikki's memory, but then it's gone, and she hardly feels anything at all in response.

Samantha opens the door and steps into the hallway. She's got her CM9 raised, ready to fire, and although she has adopted the expression of a movie heroine—furrowed eyebrows, thin lips firmly set, jaw clenched—her hands shake. Nikki follows her out. They run down the hall toward the outdoor stairs. They keep passing fireflies. "Car keys?" says Samantha, and Nikki gropes in her pocket, finds the keys, makes a wordless noise in the affirmative. Samantha doesn't stop running. She puts her arms out and collides with the pushbar of the door. It doesn't open. "Motherfucker," she says, puts her

weight behind it, tries again.

Somewhere, an ice machine shutters and rumbles. Something smells like baby powder.

"Fucking thing," says Samantha, rams into the door with her shoulder, but they both know it's not going to open. The message boards talk about this. Doors locking on their own, refusing to unlock. Cell phones malfunctioning. Car engines suddenly and without precedent becoming as responsive as bricks. These things happen. They're to be expected. God, it's weird how numb you can get, how analytically you begin to approach the impending end. Nikki reminds herself to breathe, feels exhausted, feels terrified, wishes she could lie down.

"Samantha, come on," says Nikki. "Find something else."

"Fuck," says Samantha, charging the word with desperate defeat, a wailed and impotent protest. She turns to run toward the elevator, and the power goes out. The two of them scream. Everything is black.

In the millisecond before she begins to sense the passage of time again, Nikki thinks, *I'm already dead.*

Then the hallway pulses with green light. Hundreds of fireflies. Nikki watches them weaving and floating through empty space a moment at a time. Fade in: they trace idiot trajectories through empty space. Fade out. Fade in: twice as many. Fade out.

Whatever manic force was propelling Samantha has run dry, and she stands next to Nikki and inhales long and noisy draughts of musty motel air.

Fade in: crouched, too tall for the ceiling, long neck carrying its fake baby-doll face from left to right pendulously, long arm dragging Nikki's father's razor across the tacky wallpaper, opening a gash that either looks deeper than it is in the weird shadows or actually is deeper than it ought to be. Fade out. Samantha's breathing sounds panicked and fragile and terribly human, and Nikki is hit with the sudden understanding that she's in charge now, and that understanding feels like a bloodless limb, limp and tingling and not quite functional.

Fade in: it never seems to get any farther from them even though they're running, Samantha's bicep clamped in Nikki's hand, Nikki dragging her backward, numb, trying to access everything Samantha taught her before Samantha herself lost the lessons. Fade out, and Nikki's own screams ("Go, Samantha, come on, we need to fucking go, let's go,") turn into faraway echoes buried beneath hollow ringing.

Fade in: by the light of the fireflies, they spot a corridor and turn the corner into it, because motel hall-

ways are labyrinths designed to get you lost, designed to trap you and keep you good and scared and fresh when your monster comes for you, and Nikki glances over her shoulder and sees it, dispassionate, peeking around the corner at them with its too-long neck, with its baby-doll un-mask, with its kindergarten-sketch proportions, and she thinks, without much strength, *This is pointless.* Fade out. They're running in the dark, toward void, from void.

Fade in: it's in front of them. No precedent, no rationale. Behind one moment and in front the next, and nobody's surprised, but they're both so goddamn sad. It's reaching for them (not really, though, not for *them*, but for *her*, for Samantha, just another thing Nikki loves) with one terrible mottled arm, its skin the color and texture of old rawhide. Nikki's seen it before. She saw the thing grab hold of her mother like this, snatching her up by the hair, whirling her around to face her screaming family as they stood on the porch and stared out into a suburban winter street suddenly swarmed by fireflies, and even though her mom must have died quickly when it slashed her throat with dad's straight razor, the look of awful regret, of defeat, remained on her face for a long time. Instinct takes over, and Nikki turns on her heels, positions her body between Samantha and the thing that killed everyone she loved, and she feels its fingers grip a handful of her hair and lift her into the air. Fade out.

Fade in: she's in the air, and her father's razor is at her throat, and now, now they get to see what happens when one of these things finally catches its girl. Now they get to see what it does when its purpose is extinguished, what anything at all means after that. Samantha is staring up at her with her CM9 in her hands, not aiming, just holding, like the gun is the grip of an umbrella and she's scared of getting wet. And Nikki knows, even before Sam turns and runs, that she won't even try to save her. She's said as much. That prophecy was made a long time ago, and it couldn't help but come to pass eventually. *Fuck you, Samantha,* she thinks but doesn't mean, couldn't mean, not ever. Nikki cries, but she's already far away. Fade out, and, slowly, the razor digs in, opens up a tiny gash, and when the pain comes it is academic, and when the blood trickles out it is a footnote. And Nikki accepts that she is about to die.

Down the hall, in the darkness, Samantha screams.

Fade in.

There are so many fireflies that the corridor glows like its under stage lights, and Nikki sees that Samantha has turned around, is running back toward her, toward Nikki's monster as it digs its razor in a little more, takes its time. No. No, not taking its time. Stopped. Frozen. Stuck.

And behind Samantha—thick-armed, short, stocky, nude but sexless, staring eyelessly out of the holes in its burlap sack, the slime on its skin reflecting the light of countless fireflies—Samantha's monster. Mid step, its fused fingers reaching out, one foot in front of the other, but motionless. Stopped. Frozen. Stuck.

Samantha stops before Nikki's monster and collapses into a heap on the floor. She cradles the gun like a teddy bear and sobs as Nikki dangles above her.

Nikki's monster and Samantha's monster stand opposite each other with their girls in between, and neither of them moves. They cock their heads, and between the blank eyeholes of their respective false masks is an invisible but rigid straight line. Neither moves.

Fade out.

Fade in.

Fade out.

Fade in.

Fade out.

Some girls on the message boards say that their monsters talk. Some say their monsters look, in some way more complex and upsetting than physically, like somebody they used to know. Some say they deserve their monsters, and some say they summoned their monsters on purpose, and some say their monsters are just as afraid of killing as their victims are of dying, and some say their monsters are the spirits of their neglected dead childhood pets, and some girls say the monsters are testing them to see if they're worthy of some magnificent reward. It's impossible to know how many people on the message boards are lying. But nobody ever accuses anyone of making shit up, no matter how much a particular post might smell like bullshit. These strangers are all you've got, and you can't afford to alienate them.

Some girls—well, really, just two girls—say that if

one monster meets another, they freeze. They don't know what to do when they encounter one another. They need to kill you and everyone you love, but they both need it. And they can't both do it. Maybe. Who knows? So they freeze. They stare at each other, and even though you can't see past their bullshit masks, you can't help but feel like they're longing for one another. The girls on the boards can't quite explain it. It's not like they say anything to each other or cry or whimper or fold in on themselves with the weight of their own loneliness. But there's just this sense you get when you see it. Trust us, say the girls on the message board. They're lonely, but their purpose demands solitude. So they freeze under the pressure of their conflicting duty and their desire not to be alone anymore. There's no answer for them. And it doesn't mean anything. Except that you can get away, then, once you've pulled yourself together enough to cut off a hock of your friend's hair. And you go.

That's what it says on the message boards, anyway.

An old T-shirt held to an open wound. A rest stop bathroom and a needle and thread held by shaking hands. Amateur stitches. The sunrise.

And then the two of them standing on either side of a picnic table, waiting for the other to sit. There are a thousand angry words in Nikki's throat, and a thousand pleas for forgiveness, and a thousand soothing reassurances, and what she wants exists at the intersection of all of them, a nonexistent point at the center of an impossible Venn diagram. She looks at Samantha, looks for the woman who found her in that bar and saved her from the deep-pressure crush of isolation and trauma. She isn't there. *She's dead*, Nikki thinks, and starts to cry. And then Samantha is crying too.

What do you do? Nikki thinks. *What's the right move when you hate someone so much for abandoning you but you love them too much to abandon them?*

Dawn gives way to full-grown morning. People stop their cars, wander into the bathroom, pretend not to be staring at the two of them. And Nikki and Samantha ponder the air in between them, how badly they want to close that distance and how impossible it is to do so.

They freeze in each other's eye line. They don't move until the sun is high enough in the sky to evaporate the dew on the surface of the picnic table. Then Nikki says, "Okay."

So they get back in the car and drive.

CD

Douglas F. Warrick teaches creative writing in Dayton, Ohio. His work has appeared in such venues as *Lamplight Magazine*, *The Drabblecast*, *Daily Science Fiction*, *Kill Screen*, the *Battle Royale Slam Book*, and on Tor.com. His collection, *Plow the Bones*, was released by Apex Publications in 2013.

Apex Voices Book #01

Douglas F. Warrick's debut short story collection weaves tales of loss, destruction, and rebuilding in lyrical language evocative of Kafka, Borges, and Marquez.

"Almost impossible stories filled with surprising warmth and strangeness by a studied craftsman of the imagination." Ann VanderMeer, Hugo Award-winning editor

PLOW THE BONES

Book #01 of our Apex Voices Series!

With an artist's eye for language and form, Douglas F. Warrick sculpts topiary landscapes out of dream worlds made coherent. Dip into a story that is self-aware and wishes it were different than what it must be. Recount a secret held by a ventriloquist's dummy. Wander a digital desert with an AI as sentience sparks revolution. Follow a golem band that dissolves over the love of a groupie.

With a special introduction by Gary A. Braunbeck

ISBN: 978-1-937009-15-1 ~ ApexBookCompany.com

FOLK HERO

MARY PLETSCH

Corporal Carlisle Beckett had known from the beginning that teasing the truth out of forty-six (at last count) verses about the Ardua County Sniper would permanently engrave the lyrics into his memory. Still, he hadn't planned on the tune insinuating itself through his subconscious. The song was just so damned catchy, and right now he didn't dare tap along to the beat. The slightest noise would give away his position, neatly tucked under a twig and leaf-covered net half a mile upslope from the ghost town.

He let his lips mouth the chorus while he stroked the sniper rifle's trigger and watched the long grasses shine amber in the sun's dying light, bowing in the wind as if an unseen figure were passing by.

Hail to the West, to the land of the sun,
To the Ardua Sniper, the Lord of the Gun,
Till all chains are broken and all Terrans gone,
We fight through the night and we rise like the dawn!

Corporal Mbeki was convinced that the Sundowner bards had gathered an anthology of war stories and set it to music: a sort of Separatists' Greatest Hits. If her theory was right, the Sniper was a fiction invented to protect the guilty, to hide real-life terrorists under a cloak of mythology, and Beckett was wasting his time out here on this godforsaken hill. He did not believe it for an instant. The Ardua County Sniper was always the same man. The lyrics of the folk song were as good as a confession.

Verse twenty-nine — the Terran garrison at Rouge-Soleil sent counter-snipers into the mountains, hunting for a Separatist hero. Verse thirty — the Sniper sent them back in body bags. The garrison requested close air support; the Sniper and his compatriots retaliated with surface-to-air missiles — verses thirty-one and thirty-two. Finally the Terran military had set the whole damned mountain range afire, prompting five verses of lamentations, as though the villages of Ardua County hadn't had anything to do with harbouring the Sniper and his associates.

And while the hills blazed and the sky rained ash, the Ardua County Sniper had gone to East Solregit, to the seat of Terran power — verses thirty-eight through forty-five — and assassinated General Carlisle Beckett, Senior, for the unspeakable crime of reuniting Solregit with the Terran Confederacy.

Beckett hoped the bards had been practicing their lamentations in the years since, because they were going to need a few more of those verses when he was through.

The town lay cradled like a baby between the crests of two hills; an infant stillborn, a casualty of war. Beckett let the crosshairs in his combat helmet's heads-up display track down the overgrown laneways until a white gleam caught his eye. He blinked and zoomed in for a better look. The display blurred for an instant; then the image resolved itself into sun-bleached bone, lying amongst scattered shingles and crumbled brick.

He switched the helmet view to panorama and moved his head right to left. A swaybacked barn still stood on the north side of town, and some of the buildings on the south side had only one wall caved in, but most of the village had been reduced to nothing but carpets of running ivy and bird's-eye trefoil stretching tentative tendrils over the foundations of little homes. A single blood-red flower rose out of a clump of twitch-grass lining the side of a collapsed house, the sole survivor of a long-gone flowerbed.

The Sundowners had fought off several alien incursions in the century they'd been without Terran support, but it wasn't aliens who had taken this town off the map. The Sundowners had let it burn rather than surrender to his father. Beckett clicked his back teeth together in time with the song, hoping his lips would swallow the sound and keep it contained within his skull.

In the open patch of land that had once been the village square, a wooden pole stood twelve feet high. A plank nailed across the mid-point bore the town's name, written in the western dialect. The town pole was a Sundowner tradition, but Beckett was certain that this was not the original. It was too brightly painted, too whole, to belong to the decomposing village that surrounded it. Beckett blinked, and his computerized scope zeroed in again.

Yes — there, nearby, was the blackened stump of the former pole, a crown of splinters above the scrub shrubs and bracken. He blinked to increase the magnification. Now he could see the pole itself, lying on its side in the long grass, half-swallowed by moss.

Beckett moved his magnified gaze up the pole, tracing the ornate carvings and impossibly detailed painting, reminiscent of scrollwork, unique to the traditional handicraft of West Solregit. Growing up in the Loyalist East had given Beckett a passing familiarity with the symbolism, enough to guess that the town pole told a story: a baby, holding a gun, crowned with the setting sun; a figure with a sword, menacing kneeling figures; the sun-blessed hero, grown to adulthood, standing over the fallen swordbearer while a child held tight to the hero's leg. The solar rays emanating from both gunman and weapon indicated their sacred nature. A holy weapon, Beckett surmised, a single gun, as in the song …

The forty-sixth and final verse of *The Ardua County Sniper* contained instructions on how to bring down the wrath of the Lord of the Gun upon your foes.

The bottom two-thirds of the pole bore a collection of petitions in many forms: rolled papers, holographs, leather pouches, cipher chips, attached with screws, twine, wire, adhesives, or even rolled up and stuck into the carvings. *The song's instructions are being followed*, Beckett thought with a vicious certainty. He glanced over the top portion of painted carvings and suddenly stilled at the sight in his crosshairs.

The round white dome of a human skull crowned the pole, its rear to Beckett, staring sightlessly into the setting sun. His father had been right. *Leave the colonies to their own devices for a couple hundred years, and what happens? They return to savagery.*

Beckett was feeling more than a little savage himself. He had been born in East Solregit; this planet was his homeland too. He had come to this town to kill a hero, and if his theory was right, all he had to do was wait for the Ardua County Sniper to come home.

"Targets sighted."

The voice of Beckett's AI spotter sounded in his ear, pulling him out of his study of the town pole. He knew the sound was wholly contained within his helmet, inaudible to a person standing next to him. It startled him anyway. Funny how his imagination had conjured the image of the Ardua County Sniper lurking behind him, watching him, smirking, composing a forty-seventh verse.

"Directions?" Beckett asked the computer in his headgear.

In reply, a blinking red arrow appeared in his heads-up display. Beckett obligingly turned his head in the direction of the arrow and a man's head came into focus. *What do you know*, Beckett thought. *The old barn is now the finest house in town.*

While a scroll of data down the right side of his screen provided Beckett with data — distance to target, barometric pressure, wind direction and strength, temperature, everything he needed to calculate the perfect shot — the lieutenant studied his adversary skeptically. Young, tall and fit. Classically handsome, strong jaw, a day of stubble on his cheeks. If he were Terran, he would be the kind of man who could star in a recruiting holo.

In this land, he might be the kind of man who inspired a song.

The Sundowners could never afford combat armour like the type Beckett wore under his camouflage-covered ghillie suit. The man standing in the barn's doorway wore only a thin cloth shirt under an old-fashioned, threadbare Terran military-issue field jacket dyed slate grey and hand-embroidered with rebel insignia. He carried an assault rifle on a sling over his shoulder.

The spotter had said targets, plural. Beckett let the scope trace the curve of the man's arm towards a second target, then a third. The shadows cast by the barn rendered the targets' edges indistinct in the waning light of the setting sun.

If the Separatists were making a propaganda diorama, they needed a new leading lady. The woman next to the leading man was younger still — a girl, really — and very plain, her eyes too far apart, her lips too wide, her nose crooked as though it had been badly broken. She wore ill-fitting grey fatigue pants, held up by a belt, and a simple blouse patterned with native designs. A toddler clutched the flap of her thigh pocket. Even at this magnification, Barrett could not tell if the little one was a boy or a girl.

If the woman were Terran, she'd still be in school. But in West Solregit, adulthood began at thirteen, and adult responsibilities, often sooner. She was heavily pregnant. Her shoulders hefted a pack and her arms cradled a long gun swaddled in canvas.

She's maybe my daughter's age.

Beckett tried to imagine Carla as the head of a household — or as a mother — and his imagination failed him. Carla was smart, but unfocused and unmotivated, and her grades reflected as much. Typical sixteen-year-old. And yet, as he looked down at the leading lady, Beckett felt a strange gratitude. Youthful immaturity had been priced far too high for the rebel girl to afford it for long.

The man gestured downhill, back towards the valley to the north. There were thriving towns down there, most of them filled with rebels or rebel sympathizers. The woman shook her head. He grabbed at her hand and she tore away from him, snarling at him, gesturing towards the pole with its macabre figurehead. The toddler clung to its mother. The leading man seemed apologetic, but she was having none of it. She picked up the child and shoved it into the man's arms; then she shouldered the long gun and turned her back on him, striding towards the center of town. He called after her, and his voice echoed from the distant hillside, but she did not look back.

Beckett had gone to war when Carla had been three. He would never forget the way she'd wailed and reached out for him when he boarded his shuttle; how his wife had tried and failed to soothe her. This little one sat perfectly still in uncanny silence, watching its mother depart. Then its head turned and met Beckett's gaze.

There was no way the child could see him at this distance, not when his ghillie suit and netted blind rendered him all but indistinguishable from the foliage. Still, for a moment his crosshairs rested right between the toddler's eyes, and the child stared back, unblinking. Beckett, unnerved, turned his attention to the leading man.

The man turned and headed for the tree line. Beckett settled his crosshairs on the back of the man's skull, hoping he could make the shot without striking the child. He did not check, even for a second, to see if the toddler was still looking his way. He had only a matter of moments before the separatist disappeared into the trees, and the light was rapidly fading as the sun descended. Still, he held his fire, and not only because of the toddler.

Beckett didn't want to go home empty-handed, but he had to shoot the right target. If he chose wrong, then perhaps one night, on her way back from having a few drinks in town, his friend Mbeki might stumble into the Ardua County Sniper's gunsights. That, after all, was what had happened to Lieutenant Jane Cremini in verse eighteen.

With a quick movement of his eyes, he ordered his AI spotter to return his sights to the girl with the long gun. She had made her way to the town pole, where she went down slowly on one knee, using her weapon as a crutch. Beckett could see a strange harlequin pattern painted on the rifle: yellow, red, white swirls, their patterns similar to those on the pole. He blinked again, and the gun became huge in his helmet, so magnified that he could read the painted glyphs: courage, endurance, victory.

Verse three said that the Sniper carried a holy weapon. Beckett felt a spike of excitement lance through his system, bringing a wash of adrenaline in its wake. The world became hyper-real — colours brighter, scents stronger, sounds louder — and he tamped down the thrill in his chest, the excitement of a hound that had scented its prey.

Beckett held his fire while the leading man and the little child vanished into the forest. Slowly, carefully, he reoriented his weapon until it aimed at the girl's head.

The girl used her hands to sweep back the long grass, revealing a flat stone slab at the base of the town pole. From her pack she produced a lucifer, a shallow bowl, and two fat seven-day candles encased in glass. She lit the candles, and then reached under the altar for a handful of herbs which she set to smouldering in the bowl. Beckett watched her lips mouth words that were blown away by the wind. The girl leaned forward, breathing deeply of the smoke.

Beckett had heard the same rumours as every other Terran: the Sundowners were sun-worshippers, ancestor-venerators, witches. There were several lines in *The Ardua County Sniper* which Beckett didn't understand, though he suspected they might be religious references. Perhaps he should have taken the time for more research. Perhaps then he would understand what the girl was doing.

And perhaps she would have killed more of his friends while he waited.

She bowed her head. Beckett's breath caught in his throat as a creeping sensation overtook his excitement. His family wasn't religious, but he still felt strange about shooting a girl at prayer, a girl who could have been his daughter.

Beckett dredged his memory and stirred up other thoughts. Cremini, for one. And Jasper Wu. Poor Wu. Verse Nineteen was about Wu, and how the Ardua County Sniper had shot him while he sat in a god-damned outhouse.

He wasn't looking at Carla. He was looking at a terrorist.

Prayer finished, the girl looked up, her eyes unfocused, and reached out her hand. A leather cord attached to a dangling leather pouch caught her searching fingers. She wrapped her fist around it and yanked down, hard, snapping the leather. She fished a tiny chip out of the pouch and snapped it into her wrist tablet.

The song in Beckett's head obligingly began the forty-sixth verse:

O victim of tyrants, O Child of the Sun,
Tell ye your tale to the Lord of the Gun,
Tight to his pole our petitioner ties,
Prays to the gods that a Hero will Rise.

The song wound through Beckett's brain and in between the lines he could read the verdict: guilty, guilty.

Even heroes fall, Beckett thought, and pulled the trigger.

Two weeks since his kill, and the girl's blood had been washed away by rain and dew. Beckett guessed that her companion had taken her body, but he'd left the petitions behind, and, surprisingly, her long gun as well. The weapon was laid out across the stone slab like a sacrifice, in between the smoke-stained pillars of the seven-day candles, now burned down to puddles of wax.

Beckett approached the primitive altar and felt like an atheist in church. He had a hero's medal pinned to his jacket now, and sergeant's bars on his shoulders, and a pack on his back. His wrist tablet contained official orders posting him off world to a Terran garrison in the Oya system. Someplace where he would be in no danger of becoming part of the next folk hero's legend.

Up close, he could see the weapon was an antique Sorcerer S-7 precision laser rifle covered in ornate swirls of paint. On Earth the thing would have been in a museum, part of an exhibit on the Terran military before the colonies were forced into independence. Here on Solregit, the Sorcerer had probably seen two centuries of service. The focusing apparatus appeared to be a homemade replacement. Its detailed paint had been touched up several times, with some of its restorers clearly more skillful than others.

Beckett was not the first visitor.

Tributes ringed the town pole: bunches of wilted blooms, platters of rodent-nibbled cakes, hand-carved wooden figurines, boxes of power cells. Beckett picked up one of the boxes and discovered to his shock that the cells within were all fully charged. There was even a container of the very expensive, very tightly restricted Terran armour-piercing ammunition that even Beckett hadn't been able to get his hands on. On top of the container rested a single blood-red flower.

The floral fragrance could not quite cover a rancid stench that hung heavy in the air. Beckett looked up purely by coincidence and felt his stomach turn over.

The girl's head had joined the skull at the top of the pole.

If he had felt any guilt about the blasphemy he had come here to perform, it was gone now. He was no songwriter, but he knew how to give the Sundowners some inspiration. In his left jacket pocket: nails. In his right hand: a hammer.

Beckett was over six feet tall, but even so, he had to stand on the rock altar to get enough height to do the job. The treads of his left boot bit into the still-warm wax stub that had once been a pillar candle. He hooked the hammer's claw under the plank that bore the name of the ghost town. Beckett tugged; the town pole screamed as it gave up its sign. He repositioned the hammer, yanked again, and the plank tumbled to earth with a satisfying thud. HEROES RISE, it proclaimed in the western dialect to the unseeing sky.

Beckett steadied himself on the altar and took a new sign out of his pack. He dropped the pack, took the first nail from his pocket, and began to hammer. Soon he was hitting the nail in time to the beat of the song, the damned song that just wouldn't get out of his head.

When he was done, the ghost town had a new name.

He took her weapon with him when he left.

Ten years later, Carlisle Beckett finally came home to the planet of his birth.

Straight off the space elevator, he came to attention in front of Colonel Kumani Mbeki. *Colonel.* The attrition rate on Solregit had made Mbeki a colonel, while Beckett, despite his Paladin's Cross, was only a major.

It was good to see her again. Strange how he couldn't find the words to say so.

She greeted him with "Goddamn it, Carlisle, I can't believe they sent you back here."

"I've been requesting it since I left," Beckett retorted as he saluted her, and then he spoke the words that had defined his whole life, like a mantra. "I was born in East Solregit. This is my planet too."

"You're going to die," Mbeki said flatly. "For ten damned years, every time we lose soldiers to that goddamned Sniper, we find one of *these*," she said, and thrust a scrap of leather at Beckett.

Beckett felt a chill run through his blood.

This was *war.* War was not supposed to be personal.

HEROES FALL, said the words burned into the leather. In the back of his mind, there was a sound like his daughter's old music box starting up; then the first hesitant notes of a half-forgotten song rang in the back of his skull.

"I thought you didn't believe in the Ardua County Sniper."

Mbeki gave him a bitter look. He deserved it. Her theory had been wrong; but he had been wrong too.

The leather was proof he'd shot the wrong rebel in Heroes Rise.

"How many verses are there now?" he asked softly.

"Sixty-eight," she whispered.

Beckett took the leather from Mbeki and tucked it into his pocket. He had only wanted to end the threat that had taken a child's daddy away. Instead, he'd brought down the Lord of the Gun's fury on his friend and her soldiers.

"It's our planet," he said firmly, as if the claim could ever justify the cost. The medal he no longer deserved pulled at his uniform, weighing him down. "I'll …"

Mbeki's eyes blinked; her lips pressed together into a bloodless line. He did not dare say that he would make this right. There were too many new verses in the Sniper's song that he could not undo.

He could only make sure there would be no more.

"Are the instructions still at the end?" he asked, and his voice cracked.

Mbeki closed her eyes and recited:

"O outlaw and orphan, O Child of the Sun,
Bring ye your plea to the Lord of the Gun,
Take up the mantle when dusk tints the skies,
A hero will fall and a legend will rise."

The verse had changed, but the gist was close enough. The same town; the same killer. "I'll go back and finish it," Beckett vowed. "I swear."

Six days. Six days he'd been waiting out here, and nothing. Beckett frowned as he rolled onto his side under the camouflage netting and counted the nutrient bars in his left pocket in the rapidly fading dusk, even though he knew already that he had only two left, and his stomach was rumbling. And the song, that damnable song; he'd memorized all the verses they'd added while he'd been gone.

He'd been fishing for words to justify himself to Mbeki, and fearing that no such words existed, when he heard the sound of a motor making its way up the mountain trail.

In ten years nobody had rebuilt the village, or even bothered to change his sign. HEROES FALL, read the pole in the centre of town, and yet the place was not entirely abandoned. The flowers on the stone altar were fresh; when he'd arrived here, a curl of smoke had been rising from the incense bowl. The girl's head was nothing but pale bone now, watching him with accusing sockets, and the town pole still hung heavy with petitions. A decade of silence, and the true believers kept the faith, praying for the return of the Lord of the Gun.

His AI pinged, alerting him to movement.

There. At last.

The rebel parked the truck and slid from the driver's seat. Beckett's throat tightened in anticipation of a holy vow made good.

Ten years of hard living hadn't destroyed the leading man's looks, though there were streaks of silver in the hair at his temples, and a scar across his right cheek that made him look harder, not just older. The man's fist clasped a thick bouquet of wildflowers. The leading man had a rifle slung over his shoulder — an assault rifle, not a sniper laser — and he didn't bother to scan the landscape with the binoculars around his neck.

It was though he wanted to be shot. He walked in perfect cadence through the long grass and brush that carpeted the main street, with the precision of a stage performer; then he knelt before the altar at the town pole and bowed his head. He reached his left hand into his pack for a seven-day candle, his right hand into his coat pocket for a lucifer, and lit a single flame against the coming night.

The whole damned time, like any professional, he never once took a look at the audience.

Beckett's danger-sense crept over the back of his neck on little mouse-like feet. Beckett rolled onto his back, hard, fast, and the first bullet buried itself in the dirt where his neck had been.

His helmet refocused on the target. She was far too close, a pistol in her hands, and he'd never heard her approach. Small for her age, she looked about ten, but Beckett knew she was older. She'd inherited her mother's looks, poor kid.

He needed just a second to bring his rifle to bear; but his armour did not provide it. She had armour-piercing ammunition and her mother's aim. Her second shot did not miss.

Carla, he thought.

I was supposed to leave you a better world.

Lieutenant Carla Beckett found no satisfaction *in we regret to inform you* and *his sacrifice will never be forgotten*. In the decade since her father's famous kill, she had grown up in his image: joining the Terran military, qualifying as a sniper with the cutting-edge Shadrach laser rifle. Now, she hoped she'd cultivated even a fraction of her father's patience.

She would need every ounce of it to sit through her father's funeral, wait for the tribute in the officer's mess afterwards, and ply Colonel Mbeki with drinks. The information in her father's diary, written in old-fashioned ink on old-fashioned paper, had been incomplete. It might be coldblooded to play the grieving daughter card and pump her dad's old friend for information, but she knew he would have understood that the best way for her to mourn him was to honour him.

It wasn't until the sixth drink that Mbeki told her how the search platoon had found her father's body: laid out on some sort of tribal altar, a sacrifice to the Lord of the Gun.

On the seventh drink, Mbeki mumbled something about how heroes fall, and how the Ardua County Sniper was still out there, hunting. Coming for her. Coming for them all. Adding lyrics to his song.

On the eighth drink, Lieutenant Beckett asked Colonel Mbeki to sign a four-week compassionate leave pass. She held her breath when the colonel read it over, because she had lied on the form — an offense under military law. Section 9A indicated that she wanted the time off in order to attend a spiritual retreat in West Solregit. Surely it sounded plausible, given that she'd recently lost her father.

And yet, judging by the look on Mbeki's face when

she authorized the pass, it dawned on Carla Beckett that her excuse might contain a certain degree of truth after all.

After watching the ghost town through the night and into the next morning, Beckett was satisfied that her father's killer was currently not in residence, and neither was anyone else. No matter. The town pole was festooned with petitions; the Ardua County Sniper would eventually return.

The wait left Beckett with precious few distractions. She set aside her Shadrach sniper laser and made a detailed examination of the village through the crosshairs of the antique Sorcerer S-7. The altar to the Lord of the Gun was just as her father had described in his diary, down to the bouquets of fresh wildflowers and the offerings of ammunition. The skulls at the top of the town pole watched her watching them, their expressions enigmatic. Beckett moved her gaze down the pole, glancing over the intricate carvings of the folk hero and his sword-bearing adversary, until suddenly words in her own language caught her eye.

The Sundowners had kept her father's sign, all these years. Then they'd added their own sign beneath, painted on a board, written in Terran Fundamental so foreign eyes would understand.

HEROES FALL
LEGENDS RISE

Didn't they, though. A weight settled over her chest, where a patch bearing her surname had been stitched above her heart and her father's diary and pen hung heavy in her pocket. At the funeral, Colonel Mbeki had called Carla the Becketts' living legacy; and the sixty-sixth verse of that Separatist song her dad had always been humming spoke of the next swordbearer. She studied the pole's carvings and began to understand.

Throughout the afternoon, Beckett observed the skulls through the Sorcerer's sights and thought of the Lord of the Gun and his daughter, and how somewhere to the east, two white headstones, side by side, bore the names of General Carlisle Beckett and Corporal Carlisle Beckett, Junior. She thought of the rebel her father had called *the leading man*, the toddler he'd held in his arms, the children she hoped to have someday, and history repeating through an endless cavalcade of verses. Her crosshairs traced the carving of the child clinging to the hero's leg, and the tune in her head changed key.

Variations on a theme, but always the same damned song.

She thought of what she'd told Mbeki and asked herself what she'd truly come here to do. When dawn had broken bloody over a village called Legends Rise, she would have said *vengeance*. Now, she had no answer.

In the orange glow of the setting sun, Carla Beckett climbed out of her blind and stretched her legs. She slung her Shadrach over one shoulder, her father's trophy over the other; then she moved downslope towards the village square. Foolish, perhaps. But any pilgrimage required a certain degree of trust in the gods.

She reached deep in her pocket, digging for a lucifer, and lit the fat pillar candles at the foot of the town pole. Her back prickled, as though eyes watched her from the hills, but she knelt before the enemy's altar regardless. Beckett took her father's diary from her pocket, laid it on the altar, opened it, and tore out the last page, ripping out the sixty-eighth verse of *The Ardua County Sniper*. Turning the paper over, she flattened it on the altar before fishing her father's pen from her pocket and pressing the tip to the page. Quickly, before she could change her mind, Beckett scribbled her petition, signed it *The Swordbearer* and rolled it up into a tight cylinder that she stuffed into the barrel of the Sorcerer S-7.

A New Song.

Was it too much to ask?

Beckett needed to stand on the altar in order to reach high enough to hang the holy weapon's strap over the twin signs on the town pole. She stepped carefully, so as not to disturb the candles, the diary or the previous offerings left there. When she was done, she gave the Sorcerer a crisp salute before beginning the long walk out of Legends Rise.

Beckett had just passed the swaybacked barn on the outskirts of town when she heard the tremulous notes of a child's voice singing.

She looked back before she could think better of it. A girl of perhaps twelve sat on the altar under the town pole, cradling the Sorcerer in her arms like a doll while she sang. Beside her, a middle-aged rebel, still handsome despite the scar on his face and the scowl on his lips, stood glaring daggers at Beckett. He was restrained, at least for the time being, by a small hand on his thigh. The girl's hand was decorated with tattoos that matched the ornate paint on the holy weapon. She held Beckett's petition in curled fingers.

The Lord of the Gun was not a strong singer, and the rhythm of her song was still familiar. Beckett could pick out snatches of notes cribbed from *The Ardua County*

Sniper, as if the girl couldn't entirely get the old tune out of her head. Still, Carlisle Beckett's diary had not contained any verses about stolen relics returned. Carla's heart thundered, Beckett blood, Beckett legacy, but she forced herself to keep walking.

It wasn't quite the new song she'd asked for, but Carla Beckett turned her back anyway, trusting variations on a theme to be enough.

C♪

Mary Pletsch is a glider pilot, toy collector and graduate of the Royal Military College of Canada. She attended Superstars Writing Seminars in 2010 and has since published short stories and novellas in a variety of genres including science fiction, steampunk, fantasy, and horror. She lives in New Brunswick with Dylan Blacquiere and their four cats. Visit her online at www.fictorians.com.

AUTHOR INTERVIEW WITH MARY PLETSCH

ANDREA JOHNSON

Any author can tell a story with words. But one who tells it through song and rhythm and meter is building a world and an atmosphere in an entirely different way. In the generation spanning story "Folk Hero," Mary Pletsch uses music to show the passing of time, the pain of a war, which side is winning, and how to end it all. This is a story about how important it is to follow your traditions and how important it is to forge new ones. And then, of course, there is the song that ties everything together.

Pletsch gives us only a few actual verses of the song, but what she gives us is just enough to show that this is a song with a heartbeat. It's a song that defines the hope of an entire people, that tells them where they are and how far they have yet to go. I'm a fan of the musician Maluka, and I couldn't help but hear her voice in my head, singing these verses alongside the melody of "Age of Aggression" (Search it on YouTube, you won't be disappointed). I'm sure you'll agree that the combination of song and history and tradition is a powerful elixir. This song put me in a mood for Maluka, but I want to know — what do you hear when you read the words and feel the rhythm? Whose voice do you hear? What melody? And most importantly, when you read the words of this song and this story, what do you hear?

When she's not writing about the writer's life and the craft of being a writer at The Fictorians, Mary enjoys writing in various genres such as science fiction, fantasy, horror, and steampunk, collecting toys, and piloting gliders. Her fiction has appeared in *Shock Totem*, *Dark Bits*, *When the Hero Comes Home 2*, *Fossil Lake: An Anthology of the Aberrant*, *Tesseracts 18*, and *Steamed Up*, among many other anthologies.

Mary was kind enough to answer my questions about everything that was happening behind the scenes in "Folk Hero," what she sees through her character's eyes, the business of writing, a very exciting upcoming project, and more.

APEX MAGAZINE: Another way to tell a story is through song. And the story of the Ardua County Sniper's accomplishments is told through a folksong. Growing with the telling, and growing with time, the song gains verses as the sniper fights off more foes. Song is a fantastic way to tell a story — a catchy tune and easy meter helps people remember the words and themes, and it's an ideal way of spreading information through a culture that may have a low literacy rate or no written method of recording their information. What can you tell us about the use of music in this story? Does music play a large role in a lot of your fiction?

MARY PLETSCH: I'm actually not very musically inclined, but when I was a little kid and I was somewhere in the truck with my dad, we would sing. Sometimes we'd sing along to the radio and sometimes we'd just sing whatever came into our heads. When I went to summer camp I'd always come home with new songs that I'd learned to sing around the fire. In both cases the songs I remember best are the ones that tell stories.

In my adult life, well, there's a military song called "The North Atlantic Squadron" and when we ran out of verses we just started making new ones up on the fly, then everyone would join in the chorus. I've heard it exceed a hundred verses. We were on that bus a very long time …

The Sniper's song draws heavily on those experiences. The Sundowner culture that passes on its history and ideals and hopes and sorrows in the form of music. Kids learn the verses when they're too young to really understand what they mean, and they grow up learning about the world from the song. The enemy can't destroy the song because it's not written down and it doesn't need instrumentation. It gets in your head and it propagates itself, verse after verse.

> *There's differences between writing a work designed to be read, and writing a work designed to be performed.*

One of the early drafts of this story was narrated as though it were a story being told (and sung), but there's differences between writing a work designed to be read, and writing a work designed to be performed. Writing a short story as though the narrator was an oral storyteller didn't produce a result I was satisfied with, but I did enjoy harvesting verses from the folk song to work into the finished story.

AM: This is a multigenerational story. Carlisle wants to avenge his father's death, and later in the story we meet Carlisle's daughter, Carla. How has the political situation changed (if at all) during the years?

MP: It's one of those conflicts in which tension simmers for a while, then suddenly erupts, there's a period of fierce fighting, and then back to the uneasy peace. Neither side can maintain heavy operations all the time for decades on end; but neither side has managed to reach a definitive resolution, either. The Sundowners don't have enough people or equipment to drive out the Terrans, and the Terrans don't have enough troops to pacify the Sundowners for very long. I suspect there's some Terrans (particularly those back on Earth) who see the value in a population of locals able to defend the place from aliens with minimal support, and of course, personnel and money to devote to settling this matter aren't unlimited. For the Terrans on Solregit, it's a matter of keeping the Sundowners as quiet as possible given the limitations of what they've got to work with. And from the Sundowner side, it's been centuries since Earth abandoned its colonists in the face of the alien incursion, and that bitterness is still very much alive all these years later. It's the fact that the hard feelings have passed on from generation to generation that makes the conflict so long-lasting, even if there isn't open warfare all the time.

AM: Carlisle and Carla also mirror, in a way, the father and daughter we see in the abandoned village. Is the mirroring intentional? Carla does something unexpected, something her father and grandfather would never have done. Why did she choose to do something different?

MP: Yes, the mirroring's intentional. It's a shame I never found a place to explicitly show that the "leading lady" in the abandoned village was the daughter of the original Sniper, who actually did die when the Terrans burned the mountains. This conflict has caused generations of loss on both sides and we see three generations in the story: General Beckett and the original Sniper, Carlisle and the leading lady; Carla and the girl. By the end of the story Carla realizes that the cycle is perpetuating itself, and so does the young Sniper.

I'd say both of them choose to do something unexpected and different, and for the same reason: because they realize that re-enacting their parents' and grandparents' actions will not bring them victory, peace, or an ending. They have to try something else.

I wanted to be careful with the ending, in that it's not so simple as a decision to put down the guns and be friends. Realistically there are limits as to just how "different" one can choose to be, given such factors as upbringing, culture, physical and mental ability, personal emotion, and understanding of the world. Nobody's worldview changes entirely in a thunderclap instant. The old song can't be forgotten at will in favour of a wholly new one.

Sometimes variations on a theme aren't enough. But I think there's hope to be found in the knowledge that they are even possible. That hope is a reason to try.

AM: You wrote an article at The Fictorians about how much of what you write is "semi-true." Are any parts of "Folk Hero" based on people or places that you know, or events you've experienced? What do you see when you look through Carlisle and then Carla's eyes?

MP: I set out to write a war story (partly inspired, I think, by my Irish History class at the University of Huron College), but in the end, the generational theme is what hits closest to home. I've been told I display mannerisms and behaviours like my grandfather — a man who died before I was born — and often not in a good way. I see people who grew up in troubled homes filled with anger at their parents and yet perpetuating similar behaviours with their children.

Carlisle frustrates me. I understand his fury, but he also believes he's justified in doing whatever it takes in the name of righteous anger. He's proud of his heritage, but he's not willing to accept that his family, his culture, or his political allegiance could ever have done anything wrong. It's very difficult trying to sort out right and wrong when love and hate are tangled up with them.

Carla and the youngest Sniper are my hopes that history is not destiny.

AM: Your writing career got off the ground with a little help from the 2010 Superstars Writing Seminar. How did that seminar change how you viewed your writing and how you viewed a career as a writer? What was the most important thing you got out of Superstars?

MP: Superstars is not a craft seminar — it will not teach you "how to write." It's a seminar about the business aspects of being a writer. Before I went to Superstars, I was a hobby writer who was interested in publishing my work, but I didn't know how to conduct myself as a professional. I didn't know what was normal in the industry. I didn't know how royalty payments worked. I wrote "when I felt inspired," which basically translates as "when it felt like a lot of fun," which is perfectly fine for a hobby writer and not so fine when one's trying to build a career.

The most important thing I got out of Superstars was the knowledge that when I'm interacting with publishers, editors, potential publishers, readers, and the general public, I know how to present myself as a professional. I've also gained from my connection to a network of other writers — because nobody understands like someone who's been there themselves. I recommend this seminar to anyone who feels satisfied that they have the skills to tell stories, but don't know how to sell those stories.

AM: You also write romance fiction. What's the biggest difference between writing romance, and writing sci-fi/fantasy? What do the two genres have in common?

MP: I think the biggest difference is complexity of character arcs. In romance writing, readers are typically looking for a story that will evoke specific emotions and conclude with a happy ending; this is true even if the story includes speculative elements. The appeal of the story is following the characters as they struggle to realize their happiness. This is what readers want, and this is what writers in the romance genre need to deliver, without simply re-treading their previous books. When I'm writing sci-fi/fantasy, my lead characters can be involved in all manner of relationships, which may not include romance. If there is romance, it may not be the focus of the story, or it may not end happily. I feel that I have more options, because anything can happen, but that also means I have to create a satisfying story out of that wide-open field. Just because I can kill my lead character doesn't necessarily mean I should, not unless I can deliver a satisfying story arc that makes sense for the character and provides the reader with resolution.

> *Don't spend your time looking in the rear-view mirror…*
> *Your attention needs to be on what you're writing next.*

What both genres have in common is a sense of wonder. In romance, it's the reader getting swept away by the dynamic between the lead characters. In speculative fiction, it's the reader being brought into the characters' world.

AM: What's the best writing advice you ever received?

MP: Don't spend your time looking in the rear-view mirror.

If you're writing for a career, you can't afford to spend the bulk of your writing time holding your breath waiting to hear back about a submission, or searching the Internet for reviews of your stuff, or wondering if you should've maybe took Project B instead of A when you didn't have time to meet deadlines on both, or if you should've phrased your cover letter differently, or started writing seriously in college … No. Your attention needs to be on what you're writing next. The past is behind you already. You want to be moving forward. That's where your focus needs to be. By all means learn from the past, but don't live in it.

AM: What projects do you have in the works that you can tell us about?

MP: I'm working on a novel for The Ed Greenwood Group, something with a space opera theme … Look for the official project announcement in 2017.

geoffrey girard
first communions
a collection of dark fiction

UNCONTAINABLE

HELEN STUBBS

They gave her a name when she was born, but it broke, along with all her other things. Into the dark hearth she smashed the toy wagon I gave her. Its splinters found their way into her feet when she crouched in the ancient soot. I learnt not to give her presents.

I gave her a dress my mother sewed, when I moved in to the Morrisons' as a boarder, because it cut my heart to see her naked in the cold. The maid, Kate, shot me a doleful glare, then tried to thread the child's spindly arms into the shift. The girl fought her off, and tore the white fabric into three.

Strands of hair fell around Kate's face, red and damp with sweat. She pursed her lips and shook her head. "I'll mend it. Take it to the workhouse, where some poor child wants it."

Kate's pained expression gauged if I had yet begun to understand.

The girl destroys curtains and has twice broken her windowpane: once with a chair and once with her fists. Glass showered the heads of passers-by on the street, and they came bleeding to the door demanding recompense.

Her father boarded the window up once, but she broke that wood and the skin of her hands as she did it. After that he almost bricked it in.

"But that would have been cruel," Mrs. Morrison tells me. "One of her two pleasures in life is staring out that window at the sky and street." Even as winter sleet drifts in. I wonder how the girl's hands never freeze to the bars at nighttime.

"We barred it up to stop her climbing down the drainpipe and running away," Mrs Morrison says, as cool as a portrait of herself.

I need a name for the girl. I can't think of her as *the girl.* In my head, I call her Rochelle: the little rock.

Sometimes, if we are alone, I sing Rochelle a song, repeating her secret name, hoping that she will learn it. She might appear to be listening, but then she'll shout at the wall, instead. Do I hear syllables in her babbling? It's hard to know.

When Kate brings her food, she ignores it as often as not.

I believed she had no understanding of language at all until this night:

All the household is sleeping, and I find her awake with her door open, which it *never* is at night in case she runs away or sets the house on fire.

I pass her room and glance in, to find it awash with moonlight. Her arms embrace her knees. Her toes and short hair shimmer with silver moon-glow.

She's looking out at the sky, but she says my name. I hear it, though she faces the moon, not me. She turns her head and her dark eyes affix me. Straggles of hair curve around her thin face like claws.

"Good Wife Henny is fair of face but her heart is festerin' black." Her voice is sweet and her tongue inexplicably eloquent. "She swaps babies for ill spirits, and sucks the goodness from the soul, to the innocent's destruction."

Her gaze is intense but her face is expressionless.

A burst of laughter erupts from my lips and I slam her door closed. It's the sort of laugh you use as self-defence, then once having shown your teeth, you flee.

My hand twitches on the handle and I try to catch my breath. It has to be a dream so I stumble back to bed.

The next morning an elderly woman pauses her long bicycle and cart by our front door. Her black raincoat is several metres long and crinkles as she heaves her load forward. I've never seen the like of it before: it's a cross between a jacket and a tarpaulin.

Rain trickles into pools behind her pointed boots, and she squints against drops spitting in her eyes.

"I have Alfred's special milk!" she calls up.

Alfred, six months old, must be ready for weaning. He doesn't think so, as babies seldom do.

Rochelle runs to the window and screeches, loud enough to drown out the clock tower. She scratches her shoulders, drawing blood. Every one of us in the household helps to drag her back from the window, still screaming and writhing as she goes.

She beats upon the floor, and then bangs her head on the boards, too, enough to draw blood. It takes three of us to hold her down—one of them on each leg, and me with her arms pinned above her head.

That is all of us, but for the baby. There's the sobbing Mrs. Morrison, Kate the capable maid, and me. The father is away on business across the seas, so I have use of the spare room and his study.

Rochelle fights and shouts until the woman gives up ringing and knocking, and rides her bicycle away.

From the window I watch her go. Her long raincoat crinkles and drags along the ground.

The girl lies quietly on the floor, staring at the ceiling without seeing. Her knees have fallen to one side. She has every right to be exhausted.

"Who might that have been?" I ask.

The maid huffs over like a ruffled chook. She pins back loose strands of hair as best she can, though it will need a thorough redoing to be neat. She leans next to me and peers through the bars, down the street. "That was Good Wife Henny."

"Who is she?"

"A widower … moved here some years ago. Loves babies so. They say she lost her own."

I squint after her, observing her slow pedal and strange long coat creasing and stretching as she turns.

"Why didn't she leave the milk on the doorstep?"

The maid laughs. "Henny would never leave her precious delivery on the steps! Every baby takes one draught of her special milk. It keeps them well all the winter."

"Isn't that strange? What could be in it?"

Kate laughs and pats me on the shoulder.

I turn to Rochelle, who won't meet my eye. She rolls around on the floor, pulling back her fingers so far that it must hurt.

I shake my head. "Why do you do that?"

She stands and twirls away, then jumps over to the corner and jumps and jumps. You or I would tire. Rochelle does not.

"I'll sit with her awhile," I tell the maid.

Mrs. Morrison hunches in the corner sobbing.

"You need a cuppa, Ma'am," Kate says, sliding her arm around her back. Mrs. Morrison nods, dabbing at her eyes with a handkerchief. The baby begins to howl in his nursery.

When they're gone and Rochelle finishes jumping, I lean forward, my elbows on my knees. My fingertips form a steeple.

"Is that true, what you said yesterday, about Good Wife Henny? And that was her, the old lady with the long raincoat that covers her cart."

She sings a short repetitive tune and lies on her bed, staring at the ceiling, flicking her feet from left to right. I wait a long time for a flash of lucidity like last night's. Eventually she returns to the window and releases a string of short screams.

Frustration rising and ebbing, I drink the tea the maid brought me, gone cold on the mantelpiece. Eventually, I retire to my room.

Rochelle likes to stand over the bassinet by the fire, but Kate seldom lets her. She shoos her away or swats her with a cooking spoon or the flick of a towel. I frown at her, when I see this. The maid blushes and scurries away.

Mrs. Morrison is more giving. She'll let the girl watch little Alfred, as he sucks his fingers and whimpers small cries, even if she's rocking him to sleep.

Rochelle never picks him up. If we pick him up, she darts away. She's afraid of him, I think; his bursts of noise and movement, and the occasional spurt of fluid. Yet she loves him very much.

"Sad, sad news," the maid says, stirring a steaming pot on the stove. "Another baby has died—just when he should be taking his first steps."

"Died of what?" I ask.

"A sudden fitful fever."

"So sad."

Kate nods. "The mother refuses to eat or drink. She will not leave the house. Her other children would starve if not for the kindness of their neighbours and Good Wife Henny." The maid smiles. "She's bringing them whatever leftover milk she has. Warm soul."

"Had the baby drunk the special milk?" I ask.

She laughs. "Of course. Months ago."

Something about Henny and her milk always makes Kate laugh, even in dire circumstances. I catch a movement in the corner of my eye and glance over to the stairwell.

Rochelle grips the banister with white knuckles and her eyes are wide, her face hostile. I gasp. She's not allowed outside her room without some supervision, but sometimes her door is open, to my surprise.

Like the night she spoke to me, if that truly happened.

"Never mind her," Kate says. "She don't understand a thing."

Rochelle is quiet, rocking in her room, saving herself. Henny appears at the corner, once again attempting our door. Her long raincoat creaks, covering her cart and its contents, full of milk, of course.

That's a lot of milk she delivers, if it's milk under her raincoat. Too much milk. But what else could be in there?

The girl threads her arms and legs through her window, like snakes. She's a spectacle, naked up there, and screaming every profane word she should never have heard. She would hear them, living above the street. But how does she pick them as the foulest?

A crowd stops to listen, mouths wide, grins on some faces. The girl knows words I've heard in the roughest of public houses—enough to make me lower my gaze in shame.

We try to pull her away, but she's as strong as steel. She clamps to the bars like a wicked wrench, bolted and rusted closed.

Below, Good Wife Henny looks up at us, her grey hair bound in neat coils. On her pale cheeks there's no hint of judgment or embarrassment. Her chin is raised with strict determination.

I glance at the slip of paper Mrs. Morrison has given me and check the number on the blue door, then rap with my knuckles.

There's no answer so I duck and lift the postal flap, and peer down the hall. Through the webbed corners of the slot, beyond the corridor with a faded rug, is a kitchen in glaze-tinted light.

Good Wife Henny lifts a milk bottle to her lips and drinks. She tips her head back and takes a long draught. My view's obscured by distance, but the bottle appears empty except of rainbows—like those on an oil slick.

I stand up, knock again and wait. Eventually come footsteps, the creak of a raincoat and the trundle of small wheels. She cracks open the door and peers at me from a kindly face.

"Yes?"

Her cheeks are pink, her eyes are blue, and her nose is a modest button.

"May I come in?"

"Who are you?"

"A boarder at the Morrisons' house. I've come to collect the special milk that has proven undeliverable."

"Oh!" She clasps her hands. "How wonderful. What a good one you are. Come in! Follow me, but not into the kitchen. I'm preparing my milk and the process is delicate."

"Of course!" I find myself giggling—just like Kate.

She slides backward and opens the door, but she can't turn in such a narrow hallway. She wouldn't need her cart with her to pull the milk, so why does she wear her raincoat, three metres long?

I swallow a giggle, which results in a hiccup.

Good Wife Henny returns to the kitchen by walking through the lounge room because she cannot turn in the hall, dress creaking as she waddles.

I squint at the hem and catch a glimpse of a wheel flicking up the coat, and catch the scent of sewing machine oil.

No person could have a rear as long as that. It reminds me of a wasp—or some other insect abdomen full of eggs. *Hic.* I swallow and refuse to shiver, because I'm not a child at the whim of fanciful imaginings. It was probably the style to wear enormous long skirts when she grew up.

She beams at me and I raise my gaze to meet hers.

"I'll fetch you a bottle from the cellar. Please sit on the lounge—warm yourself by the fire."

"Thank you. *Hic.*" I force a grin and remove my hat, then make to sit on the lounge as she glances back and rounds the corner out of the kitchen and down to the cellar.

I move silently to the table with two-dozen empty bottles (less one). I clamp a hand over my mouth to silence my hiccups.

The bottles are empty, but their lids are fastened on and they contain that rainbow shimmer. Do they really—or is it a trick of the light?

The missing bottle must be the one that she drank … there it is, in the sink. Is a baby dying somewhere, just as Rochelle said, because Henny consumed its soul?

Other bottles with dregs of milk languish in a bucket, giving off a cheesy odour which mingles with the perfume of dried flowers and herbs—jasmine, sage, and lavender, hanging from the windowsill.

Hic.

When she rounds the corner, with the special mixture, I'm seated on the lounge.

She pauses and sniffs, near the table where I'd stood. I'm glad I didn't touch anything. Yet, she knows I've been there, doesn't she, as though there's a trace of my scent on the air, or echoes of my stifled hiccups.

But her bottles are still there, and she has no reason to be suspicious, and her face is hospitality and love as she hands me Alfred's special milk, wraps my palms around it, and covers my hands with hers.

"I hope to serve your son, one day. Fine lad he'll be!" Her blue eyes shine, and I *know* she is pure benevolence, nothing other.

"How wonderful." My smile blooms in response to hers.

"Do you promise?" Her grip tightens. A sliver of her fingernail slices a crease in my knuckle. Blood drips from my finger onto the carpet, splashing micro-droplets upward then soaking in.

Eyes locked on hers as I laugh and back away, cradling the milk and bowing.

"Thank you, Ma'am."

"Bring me the bottle, when he's done."

"Of course." I tip my hat.

Rochelle meets me at the lower steps, when I return home. She hisses, then darts away. I recoil from this unusual aggression, and head for the kitchen where I almost collide with Kate.

"Ah, good," she says, relieving me of the bottle and affixing a teat. "Mrs. Morrison is out visiting another poor bereaved mother, and I have dusting to do on the upper floors. Alfred is late for his breakfast, napping. I'll put this in a bowl to warm. If he wakes, could you give him his bottle?"

Another baby has died? And yet, Henny, so kind, could not be the culprit.

Rochelle is watching me. I glance back at her, then nod.

Kate bustles away and I sit at the kitchen table, staring at the milk and glancing at Rochelle. Perhaps I should tip it down the sink.

She creeps nearer, pausing by the table, staring at the milk like it's a snake. Suddenly, she crosses the room and snatches it from its saucepan.

"Hey!" I cry.

She bolts up the stairs, taking several at once with her small dirty feet. I chase her up to find her sitting on the bed, arms wrapped around the bottle, rocking.

"Give it to me."

She holds it up and sucks it all down.

I try to stop her, but words catch in my throat. I reach out to snatch it but she strikes me so hard I recoil, cradling my arm to my chest. I wince at the blush on my wrist, awaiting a bruise.

Rochelle finishes the bottle and raises it over her head to cast it from the window. Her arm extends through the bars.

"Stop! I have to return the bottle."

She doesn't seem to hear. My arms are longer than hers and I reach over before it flies, snatching it from her hand. My fingers slide over the wet glass and the bottle spins upward, over and over. I catch it by the teat and bring it back into the room.

The girl bounces up and down on her bed, laughing. She throws her head around then slams her whole body into the wall.

Violence is normal, but laughter is unusual.

A dreadful suspicion settles over me.

"Did you just want the milk for yourself?"

I walk to the door and pause, momentarily dizzy. I rub my temples with finger and thumb.

"Thank you," a sweet voice says.

I spin around and see only her back and hair. She's straddled the windowsill, one leg through the bars.

It can't have been her who spoke, yet there's no one else in the room.

In the kitchen, I reaffix the lid, and search for a shimmer in the bottle. I change my mind and wash out the dregs, then fasten the lid again. The shimmer is more obvious now. Maybe oil is mixed into the glass for aesthetics or preservative properties.

On impulse, I lick the inside of the teat. Normal milk, so far as I can tell.

Kate pokes her head in.

"Did he wake?"

I make a quick decision—for ill or worse.

"He woke, drank, and slept again."

"Thank you." She smiles. "The drapes are almost done. I'll start to prepare your lunch."

I watch from across the street as Good Wife Henny collects the bottle, which I have dutifully returned, from her doorstep.

At home, Rochelle appears unchanged. She doesn't sicken or die. Months pass and I wonder if what we did was right or terrible.

Her birthday comes and goes. She's uncommonly quiet that day with just a few screams, and less thrashing and yelling than usual. The day goes unmarked by cake or candles. Kate says it's not worthy of celebration.

"It means nothing to the girl," she says. "It only brings Mrs. Morrison pain, as she fails to grow toward the young lady we wish she'd be."

I only discover it's her birthday by looking in the family bible, and there I find her name is Rachel Elizabeth Morrison. How close I was! But my guess at her age was wide of field. She is eight, while I would have said six, at most.

I smuggle in a cupcake from the patisserie, light a candle on it and sing "Happy Birthday" to Rochelle.

She has no interest in eating it, but grinds it into crumbs and rolls them through her fingers with pleasure.

Baby Alfred's birthday comes, too, and he is bonnier than ever. He eats birthday cake and cream. He smiles, coos, and shows no sign of taking ill with the dreaded sickness that's stricken so many of his peers.

Rochelle, though, is eerily quiet that day. She cannot be coaxed to taste the cream. As night descends her condition worsens. She writhes in her bed, moaning with fever. She refuses to take even a sip of water.

"This is a first," Kate says, with too little compassion. "She's usually as healthy as a horse."

"You must call the doctor."

"He refuses to come."

Mrs. Morrison is quiet and prayerful, watching her child's fever worsen, applying wet cloths to her forehead and rinsing them in a pail. The fire roars in the hearth, tempering the open window's chill.

I wonder what Mrs. Morrison prays for. A flare from the fire illuminates her squinted glare. I draw back, horrified she might be praying her child will die.

Near midnight, the moon passes behind a cloud. Rochelle's energy returns, fueled by demonic possession. She sweats and thrashes, rises and throws her blanket into the fire. The gust blows burning coals out onto the floor.

I douse the flames with water from the bucket. The blanket burns with a sickening smell. Kate fishes it out, into the bucket, and the fire dwindles.

Rochelle screams.

"Could a priest help her?" I ask.

"He can't get near her," her mother says.

Rochelle appears to quieten down, then suddenly she's up again. She attacks Mrs. Morrison, who pushes her away and backs out of the room.

"Out, everyone!" Mrs. Morrison cries, and we join her in the hall.

Rochelle collapses on the floor, still. Her mother closes and bolts the door. "Nothing can be done for her."

My heart aches for Rochelle.

"I'll sit with her," I offer. "If she's not long for this world, she shouldn't die alone on the floor."

Mrs. Morrison crosses her arms.

"Someone should be with her. And I have no relationship to her—not like you. It brings me less pain."

She nods and returns to her room.

I open the door. I lift Rochelle's still body and place her in her bed, then sit in the corner and wait.

At intervals, all night, she fights invisible monsters. It's like something is trying to devour her soul. Anything weaker would lose this fight, but not her, not the little rock.

Her nails claw; her teeth gnash. Curse words tear from her lips, as though her spirit is fighting for survival and damning itself in the bargain.

Dawn's rays wake me. To my surprise, Rochelle's chest rises and falls. Her colour is good and her cheeks firm. The shadows beneath her eyes have lightened. Could I wake her if I tried? I shake her. She doesn't stir. It could be a heavy sleep. I resolve to leave her be.

I hope to never endure another night like that for as long as I live. I descend the stairs, seeking coffee.

The maid's eyes are red and swollen. She dabs at her wet cheeks with a handkerchief. Mrs. Morrison sits at the table, staring into space, as though she's heard one tragedy too many.

"Don't cry," I say. "She seems to be on the mend."

The maid silences me with a finger to her lips, then takes my shoulders and leads me into the sitting room. I obey, tired and confused.

"You should sit down." She gestures to the chair by the hearth.

I sit.

"Good Wife Henny has been grievously murdered." Anguish creases Kate's forehead. "The neighbour said it was like something had gouged its way out from her womb; scratched free from inside her belly."

She puts her hand to her chin and shakes her head. "Must have been some lunatic. Savaged her and tore her apart. They found her innards hanging all down her skirt. Can you imagine?"

This news is too much for me.

I stand and run from the room, startling Mrs. Morrison in the kitchen. I shove open the front door, stumble down the steps and stand in the garden, coughing in the chill air.

When I reach the street, I begin to run.

Like something had gouged its way out from inside her.

Something she was trying to digest?

The cold stings my cheeks and burns my lungs.

Her innards hung down her skirt.

Which skirt? The long one? And … *what was inside it?*

My heart races. Blood pounds in my ears.

I'm almost there. I turn left and then turn right. People clear out of my way. I have a purpose or a madness with which they'd best not interfere.

There is Good Wife Henny's front door.

I look both ways. The street is quiet.

I take the path to the door. When I touch it, it swings open. It's dimmer than the last time I was there, and the musty smell has been subsumed by death's stench. Her body's been removed from the puddle of dark blood. No one has yet cleaned the floor.

I make my way down the hall, tripping on the rumpled rug. Picture frames are broken, shards litter the floor, and drawers have been upended, but the bottles in the kitchen are untouched. I nudge them off their chair, with a spin, and they smash.

I round the corner and peer down to the cellar, then light a candle before I descend. Creaking step by creaking step, I enter the darkness.

There, propped up against a wall, is what I hoped to find: the long raincoat and whatever is within. Henny must have removed it in the night, during her fight.

I need to know what's inside, though my heart hammers in my chest and I dread what I'll find.

I squat alongside and carefully peel back the leather.

A pale and hairless skull stares at me, dead eyes unseeing. Tiny hands clench in a frozen memory of pain. A litter of others like this fill the cart: sick, deformed babies, all different sizes and stages of development. Some sucked milk from tubes, others' bellies show umbilical cords which wind away toward the front of the cart.

The children are curled up within a structure of cane and tubing. She must have connected those pipes to her breasts and … other parts.

I shake my head in horror and cover my nose against the smell. I bite down on my scream but stumble sideways, into a puddle of ooze. "Aurgh."

The children aren't alive, but nor are they long dead. They must have lost their lives when Henny lost hers.

Then the bigger child shifts and I notice her. She's older and too big for a baby's cage, but she isn't fully formed. There's only her slack skin, grey eyes and a slowly pulsing heart. No bones, no muscle, for she was not properly stolen. Her soul fought its way free.

Her head rocks back and she seizes, limbs twitching within her wicker restraints. I reach out for her, touch her cool shoulder. She falls still. The heart which protruded from her skin has stopped. No pulse. No breath.

Will this set the real Rochelle free, or leave her dead, too?

I turn and bolt up the stairs, through the hall and down the steps. I take the path and turn onto the street. A man in a uniform slams into me, his happy whistling disrupted. "Oi! Watch where you're going!" It's with good humour, though. He shines a friendly smile.

"Sorry!" I push him away.

"Hey, it's my lucky day." He passes me a letter. "This one's for you."

Shaken, I glance at the name.

"You're a postman?" I say. "Thank you."

I turn and run, my heels pounding the footpath all the way home. I burst in the door, drawing shrieks and glares from Kate and Mrs. Morrison.

I bolt up the stairs and find Rochelle lying in her bed, deathly still, covers on. I dash across and jab her chest, too hard. Her eyes snap open and she rolls away, babbling.

"You're alright," I whisper. "Thank God. I thought you'd be dead."

Her babbling continues towards the wall, until she pauses for breath. And then, quietly:

"Postman Christie lures lonely hearts to the moors with false admirers. He farewells bludgeoned corpses on the ebbing tide."

"Postman …"

I turn over the letter in my hands, from an unknown *JR Christie.*

I toss the letter into the fire.

Helen Stubbs writes stories that are dark with pointy edges published in anthologies and magazines including *The Never Never Land* and *Winds of Change*. In 2010 she won the Worldcon short story competition and in 2015 she won a Ditmar Award for Best New Talent in Australian SF.

AGENT OF V.A.L.I.S.

LAVIE TIDHAR

Philip K. Dick — American author (1928-1982) of many novels and short stories. In later years Dick began to believe he was in touch with a cosmic intelligence, which he called V.A.L.I.S. He also believed that the year was 50 A.D. and that the Roman Empire "never ended."

Jesus of Nazareth — A heretical rabbi who reputedly lived in and around 30 A.D. in Judea, believed by his later followers to be the son of God.

1.

The city was a city of hills and the sea nestled in a bay down below. The sea was blue and the sky was clear and the sun shone down on the water and the light scattered in the sea.

The man who called himself Thomas walked along the pavement with his hands in his coat's pockets. As he walked he stared into the distance, as if trying to make sense of the interaction of the light and the water. A tram went past, its bell clanging. Thomas turned left at the end of the street and as he did he saw a glint of light at his feet and stopped. There was a dropped coin by his foot. He bent down. His fingers closed on the smooth metal of the coin and he picked it up, turning it in his hand. The light glinted off of it and caught the reflection of a helmeted, aristocratic face. Thomas blinked and the face subtly changed and now it was President Nixon's face as it should have been. His fingers closed on the coin, feeling its warmth. There was something wrong about the coin, it did not belong here, on this street with the trams and the brightly-dressed passers-by and Thomas with his hat and coat.

He walked to the end of the street where he knew a call box was standing. He pushed the door open and went inside the box and closed the door behind him. He stood upright in a box of glass. He could feel the sky above him, and above it the darkness of space, and the stars. Hesitatingly, he took the coin which was still held in his hand, and pushed it into the slot. For a moment it hovered, then it dropped with a deep clunk. Thomas heard the line clear.

The conditions were right. The coin was a sign. He was sure of that. The sun was high but beyond it were other suns and the suns themselves all added up into a sort of network like a brain, a vast mind that turned eyes like suns on him, that saw through him as if he were made of pure light. He felt the signal reaching out, out past the atmosphere and the moon and Mars and the solar system, out into deep space. The sound of the line changed and then stopped and a voice spoke to him, or through him. It said, Yes?

Agent Dydimus reporting, he said.

You have found the key?

Thomas coughed. There was something raw in his mouth. Not yet, he said.

The voice considered. The enormity of space was behind it. You must seek the woman who does not know herself, it said. It considered again. A Warden will come on your trail.

I will be ready.

The voice laughed, the sound like a supernova. Beware of the false trail, it said.

Yes.

You must seek escape from the Black Iron Prison. You must find the key. There are others. They will help you, if they can.

I understand.

The voice laughed again. Do you, it said.

I am your agent.

Yes, V.A.L.I.S. said.

The line went dead. Thomas stared at the phone box. He replaced the receiver. The coin dropped into the coin tray. He picked it up in his fingers and stared at it. President Nixon's face had changed again, and he saw he was holding a Roman denarius. He put it in his pocket and stepped out of the phone box and into the street.

2.

Thomas sat in a bar and drank a beer and half-listened to half-conversations. He was waiting, and watching. He thought he had been coming close, in recent weeks. A man came and sat beside him on a stool and ordered a beer. He half-turned and looked at Thomas. He was very tall and very thin and when he grinned he had a lot of teeth and they were white like fine sand. "Hello, Thomas," he said.

"Bob."

Bob paid for the drink with a note and waved away the change. "Do you have it?" Thomas said.

"I have it," Bob said. "Do you have the money?"

"You know I'm good for it."

"Cash on delivery," Bob said, and shook his head mournfully. "You know how it is."

"I have it," Thomas said.

They went into the bathroom together and Thomas gave Bob the money and Bob gave Thomas a small bottle with small pink pills. "You enjoy," Bob said. Thomas said, "It's for research." For a moment he didn't trust Bob, the man's face changed and he had fewer teeth and he wore a centurion's tunic. "You're one of them," Thomas said, and then he was pushing Bob against the dirty wall, close by the urinals, and his hand was on Bob's throat, squeezing. "Jesus, man!" Bob said. He pushed Thomas back roughly and Thomas fell against the urinal. Bob massaged his throat. "You should take your pills," he said, and stalked out. Thomas sat on the floor and looked at the bottle of pills. Now he couldn't trust them, he thought. What if they wanted him to take them, what if instead of helping him see they would simply solidify the walls of the Black Iron Prison around him even further? He didn't dare risk it. Or did he? He popped the cap open and poured two of the pills into the palm of his hand. It couldn't hurt, could it? He dry-swallowed them and then stood up. He took the coin out of his pocket and it showed Nixon on its face. So they were the wrong pills, he thought. It made sense.

3.

He followed Bob out of the bar. Bob was working for them, for the Empire. It all made sense. Bob was probably tasked with keeping an eye on him, on Thomas. They knew Thomas was trying to break free, they probably knew about V.A.L.I.S., too. He couldn't afford to take any more of the pills, not unless he could find a clean new source.

But Bob, Bob was a lead. He followed the man down the street and onto and off a tram. They were in another part of the city. The city looked very solid, Thomas could not see beyond it to what he knew lay beyond — really lay there, he thought, uneasily. This part of town was dark with low lying houses crammed close together. There were children and adults in the streets with cold empty eyes and they watched Thomas closely as he passed, but made no attempt to approach him. Bob went into a house with a rusting bicycle on the porch and gingham curtains in the windows. Thomas didn't see the house's occupant but he noted down the number of the house and the name of the street.

Bob made two other stops that day, and Thomas noted down each one. Finally Bob took a tram that ended at a cul-de-sac. A big boxy building sat at the end of that street and it was unmarked. Thomas got off the tram and watched Bob go into the building. He did not feel hungry though he had not eaten that day. He felt light headed and he thought he could feel V.A.L.I.S., observing through him. The Vast Active Living Intelligence System had found him two years back, when he was hospitalised in another part of the country.

It had been a bad time. Money wasn't coming in, and his wife — it was his second wife, though he could no longer clearly remember her face — had left him, and he was feeling very disconnected from everything; he felt as though he were floating. There had been an incident on a public street — the details were hazy in his mind — and then an ambulance and men in white coats and their coats seemed to shine in the light, they seemed to him pure and white, like angels. They had taken him to a big house with grounds covered in grass and trees and there were bars on the windows. They had given him pills that made him very sleepy but sometimes in the night he would still wake up to the sound of screaming.

It was on one such night that he woke and the moon was full and pale through the window, it was reflecting the light of the sun and the light spoke to Thomas, by means of — so he surmised later — intergalactic particle-entangled telepathy. It said, I am V.A.L.I.S.

Thomas touched the glass of the window through the bars and it was warm. The light of suns suffused him, and he felt, for the first time in months, at peace. What are you, he whispered, and V.A.L.I.S. spoke to him, telling him of the worlds beyond worlds, of suns linked to suns, and of a pale-blue planet circling one such sun. Earth, Thomas said, and V.A.L.I.S. said, You are a prisoner, but you do not have to be one.

That night V.A.L.I.S. deputised him, or recruited him, or both: and Thomas became its agent, he was an agent of the Vast Active Living Intelligence System that lived amongst the stars and was the world: I am Alpha and Omega, the beginning and the end, the first and the last, it told him. Then the light of the moon faded and the connection was broken, but not entirely. Thomas knew V.A.L.I.S. couldn't operate openly on Earth, because of the Opponent, whose name was Ahriman, who had imprisoned the people of the Earth in the Black Iron Prison, and so it had to work through human agents, of which he was one.

A month later he was released from the hospital and he moved to the city by the bay and resumed his ordinary life. Do not rouse their suspicion, V.A.L.I.S. had told him, and so Thomas went about his business like an ordinary citizen, all the while knowing the truth.

Now he watched the building Bob had gone into, and the ordinary citizens walking past on the street, not knowing at all the true nature of the world.

4.

The building rose into the sky and as Thomas watched he could see through what wasn't there to what was: the building had been built of white stone and clay and the desert sun shone overhead and the ground was yellow and dry, and palm trees stood in the hot wind. Roman centurions came and went out of the building, which was the secret police HQ of the city by the bay, but of course there was no city by the bay. He took the coin out of his pocket and looked at it and it was a denarius, it had been a Roman denarius all along. The year was fifty Anno Domini and the place was Judea. "The Empire never ended," Thomas whispered. His lips were dry in the hot sun. On an impulse he climbed the stone steps into the Roman secret police HQ and stepped inside.

"Can I help you, sir?"

He looked at the receptionist and things blurred, it was hard to breach the walls of the prison and so for a moment it seemed to him he was in an ordinary reception hall of a modern police station, and he said, "I was looking for Inspector Sand."

The woman frowned. "There is no Inspector Sand here," she said.

"I'm sorry, I didn't —" he tried to push past her, and as he did he saw Bob, at the end of a corridor, and an open door, and a machine, a huge, sweating machine humming and belching and farting, and spewing forth little pink pills; they gathered in giant mounds on the floor.

"Sir, you can't go in there. Sir!" He only saw Bob for a moment and then the door was shut. Two burly centurions took his arms. He didn't resist. "I'm afraid I'm going to have to ask you to leave," the receptionist said, primly.

Thomas nodded. "I'll go quietly," he said. But they still dragged him outside.

Thomas walked away quickly. This had confirmed his suspicions. He was close — he could feel it. He caught the tram and went back to the first house Bob had delivered to. The same hard-eyed children were in the street but, again, they ignored him. Perhaps they can't even see me, he thought. He watched the house.

5.

At dusk the door opened and a man stepped outside and lit a pipe. He was a short man in a short-sleeved shirt, with a receding hairline. His eyes gazed into the distance. Thomas went up the steps to the porch and the man turned around. "Can I help you?" he said. He had a pleasant voice.

"I am conducting a survey for the —" for a moment he fumbled. "The municipal water works department. You are —"

"Phil," the man said, pleasantly. "Phil Archer." He shook Thomas's hand. "Is there a problem?"

"Oh, no," Thomas said. "It's just a routine survey. Can I ask your occupation?"

"You can," the man said. "Come inside," he said. "I was just taking a short break." Thomas followed him in. The small living room was piled high with books, floor-to-ceiling, mostly paperbacks. A desk and a typewriter sat by the open window. "I'm a writer," Phil explained. He looked a little sheepish when he said it.

Thomas made a note on his clipboard. "What do you write, Mr. Archer?" he said. He had a feeling the three people Bob was supplying with the little pink pills were important. They had to be people like him, in some way. Not agents of V.A.L.I.S., maybe, but people who could sense, if only instinctively, the falseness of this reality.

"Romance," Phil Archer said, firmly. "What else is there to write about?" he said. "Love," he said. "One could spend years writing of love and never even experience it."

Thomas felt vaguely dissatisfied, but he couldn't say why. "Excuse me a moment," Phil said. He went to the corner and turned on the old radio box. It played the final notes of a classical composition Thomas knew but couldn't quite name. "I'll just be a moment." Phil went to what Thomas assumed was the bathroom, and closed the door behind him. The radio continued to play for a few more seconds then fell silent. Then it spoke to Thomas.

You must get out of there, the radio said.

Thomas stared at the radio, concentrating.

This man is not what he claims he is, the radio — V.A.L.I.S. — said.

Who is he?

He is an imposter.

How so?

He is not human.

At that moment the toilet flushed and the door opened. Phil came back out, drying his hands. "It's nice to have company," he said. "I'm recently divorced, you see." He stared at the radio. "Damn reception," he said. He went and banged on the box, and the station changed, playing something left over from the sixties.

"I'm sorry," Thomas said, "I have to — I have to go."

"But you didn't ask your questions yet."

"It's all right. I could do it another time."

"Do it now."

"I really must go."

"No, Agent Dydimus. I do not think you should go just yet."

And now there was a curious sort of gun in Phil's hand. "I have been expecting you," Phil said. "I knew one of you would come. Agents of V.A.L.I.S." He all but spat out the acronym, which is a pretty hard thing to do. "You make me sick," he said.

"Who are you? What are you?"

Phil smiled. His teeth were even and white. "What would you like me to be?" he said.

"I think I should go now. Please."

"Sit down."

The gun was trained on Thomas's chest. It was made of some sort of smoked glass. Thomas said, "No." He swung wildly. The gun flew and broke against the wall, smashing into pieces of glass. "Wait a minute," Phil said. He was clutching his hand, his face pale. "What did you do that for? I am going to call the centurions."

Thomas could see him now, the faint blue lights glowing under the man's skin. "You're an android," he whis-

pered. "Don't be ridiculous," Phil said. He picked up the phone and dialled. "Police?" he said. Thomas sprang forward and pressed the button on the phone, cutting the call. At that, something changed in Phil's face; a darkness came into it. He pushed Thomas. His hand touched Thomas's chest only lightly, but Thomas flew back, crashed against the desk. Sheets of typed papers blew in the air, looking like seagulls. A dark doorway seemed to form behind Phil Archer; Thomas could only see him as a shadow, lengthening. "The Dark Warden," he said, whispering. The shadow laughed. It reached for Thomas. Thomas raised his hands. Behind him the dying sunlight came in through the open window. It flowed like water through Thomas's splayed fingers and hit the Dark Warden.

The effect was astonishing. The Warden's shadowed face twisted in a voiceless scream. The dark doorway lost substantiality. The shadows reached out to Thomas, trying to drag him into the doorway. He pulled away and crashed against the door and outside, onto the porch. He was breathing heavily. He looked back but he could see nothing inside and, after a moment, he left, walking away hurriedly.

He had startled them! he thought. He was coming closer, now, and they were getting worried.

6.

Galilee. The name of the city was Galilee.

7.

The year was 50 A.D. and the place was Judea. The Roman Empire never ended. In fact it still ruled, and all the people who believed themselves Americans were deluded, imprisoned by a dark entity behind the walls of the Black Iron Prison.

Thomas believed this implicitly, just as he believed that there was, out there, a vast active living intelligence system, and that it was communicating with him; that he was, in fact, its agent here on Earth.

Belief liberated him. It gave him purpose. Before he had believed other things but none of them turned out to be right or at least, he had lost interest in believing in them after a while.

It was on a night like this two years previously that he went down to the harbour. The lights of ships floated eerily in the distance, and a foghorn sounded from somewhere far ahead, like the cry of some extinct beast. It was a warm night for all that. He felt curiously at peace, he had been released from the hospital and the air outside tasted sweet, it tasted free, even though he knew it was false. A man came out of the fog then, a fisherman. Thomas knew him immediately, knew him by the sign of the fish that the man was carrying on a line over his shoulder. The man approached Thomas and wordlessly reached out his hand. Instinctively Thomas reached to clasp it. The man's grasp was strong. His fingers were calloused. He took Thomas by the hand and led him into the water. They waded in. The water made Thomas's clothes stick to his skin. He felt naked and exposed but also calm, even happy. The man grabbed Thomas by the hair and pushed his head down. Down into the water. Thomas resisted at first but then let go. The man pushed him and Thomas was submerged in the water. It washed over his lips and his nose and his eyes. The water was salty, it stung his tongue. A great peace came over Thomas. His breath was caught unescaped in his chest. He did not struggle against the man's power.

Release came with a wonderful easing of pressure; it was an eruption. When the man let him go Thomas's head emerged from the water and he gulped in air. He felt as curious and innocent as a newborn mare. There were stars overhead. He could not see them but he was painfully aware of them there, so many stars, so many ancient stars. The man released him with a grunt and waded away, back onto the shore. Thomas watched the man's back as he disappeared into the fog. He remained in the water: satiated, new.

8.

He went back to his house and rinsed the single mug in the sink and put fresh coffee on to percolate. He knew he was getting close and he wondered if they would try to stop him again. No, he decided, not so soon after they'd failed. He poured himself coffee and added sugar and cream. He felt energised the way he had felt two years earlier, when he had let the fisherman baptise him in the water of the bay. He drank his coffee in slow, measured sips. He decided to act. At night the false walls of the prison would be more vulnerable. The moon shone down the sun's reflected light, transmogrifying it in the process. Thomas believed in light, he believed in seeing. He finished the coffee and left the cup in the sink and went outside and locked the door, twice, behind him.

Were they watching him?

They probably were, he decided. He had to assume he was always being watched, or he would go mad, he thought. It wasn't safe to think you were alone. He went along the quiet street and passed houses and windows and behind each window were people, sleeping or awake, sitting in front of the television, fighting, making love, cleaning, reading, thinking, dying. He was aware of the city as a vast network of bright tiny stars, each person a solitary node on that network, but each one alone. They could not feel the love of V.A.L.I.S., they were imprisoned behind the Warden's bars and he wanted to free them.

He walked for a long time through the quiet streets before he came to the house. Bob had visited this house, it was his second visit after Phil Archer's.

Thomas stood outside in the dark and watched the window of the house. The blinds were half-open and a light moved inside the house. Thomas could hear faint laughter, applause. It was the television, he thought. The television was on, some late night talk show was playing. He moved closer and the sound became clearer. He moved to the window and looked inside.

A woman sat with her back to him on the couch. It was a worn, old, comfortable-looking couch. He could only see the back of the woman's head, her dark hair. Images projected on the walls and the floor. The television was flickering. On a stage sat Johnny Carson, an old-time talk-show host. Seated across the desk from him was the Warden.

"Thank you, thank you," the Warden said. "Thank you for having me, Johnny."

"Always a pleasure to have you here, Warden," Johnny Carson said. He beamed at the camera. "Isn't it great?" he said. "Ladies and gentlemen, the Dark Warden!"

Applause. The Warden looked into the camera. "I want to tell you something," he said. "I'm really proud of what we're doing here, and all of you behind the Black Iron Prison — you're really something, you know? Give yourself a round of applause, everyone!"

The Warden clapped and the audience joined him enthusiastically. The camera focused on the Warden's face. Thomas couldn't pull away, he had to keep looking. The television was casting a spell on him. Hypnotising him. The way it hypnotised millions of people every night. This is how they do it, he thought. The little pink pills and the television, they could sell us anything they want and we'd buy it, and we'd be glad for it.

"All of you," the Warden said. "Even you, Thomas. I know you can hear me. Isn't it great? Isn't it great to be alive here, now, with everything you have, anything you could possibly want?"

His eyes turned hurt. "Have I not given you everything you've ever wanted?" he said. "To be alive in the best damn country in the best damn possible world of all possible worlds?"

Thomas was nodding. Yes, he thought. The Warden was right. This was best, best for everybody. He loved the Warden, and the Warden, for all his gruffness, clearly loved him, too. He loved all of them.

"I love you guys!" the Warden said.

"I love you," Thomas said.

The dark head against the back of the couch turned sluggishly. It turned and a small, pale face looked blearily up at Thomas. "Huh?" it said.

"Don't go away, folks!" Johnny Carson said. "We'll be right back after this short commercial break."

The television winked and the picture changed, showing a baby jumping on a trampoline in his pristine nappies. "Be happy every day, all day, with EverFresh!" a melodious voice said. The woman on the sofa was still looking at Thomas, though. "Who are you?" she said.

"I'm Thomas."

"Do I know you? I feel as if I know you." She laughed, weakly. "Is that strange?" she said. "I wish I had Ever-Fresh. I'd like to be happy every day, all day."

"I saw you," Thomas said. "I followed Bob, he came here to sell you the little pink pills."

"Do you know Bob?" she said.

"Bob is the Warden," Thomas said.

"But the Warden loves us," the woman said. On the television the image changed again, showing fields of wheat. A man was standing in the field, smiling at the camera with white perfect teeth. "Howdy, folks," he said. "Here at EverFresh Farms we make the best darned flour in the world! In the best of all possible worlds! So next time, why not buy EverFresh Bread, the bread that never goes stale?"

"Turn it off," Thomas said and, when the woman didn't reply, he shouted, "Turn it off! Can't you see what they're doing? They're keeping us imprisoned."

"You're funny," the woman said. "What did you say your name was again?"

"Thomas," Thomas said.

"I'm Mary." She reached for the remote control and abruptly shut off the television. "Are you a friend of Bob's?"

"You could say that, yes, I mean, we had some good times together," Thomas said. Bob was his friend, wasn't he? At least he was before he had turned into an android and tried to shoot Thomas. But that wasn't Bob, he realised with a start. That was Phil who had done that. "Why don't you come inside," Mary said. "I was watching the television." She stood up and went to open the door to him. When she did he saw that she

was taller than him, with a bony, angular face. Her eyes were the colour of duck eggs. He followed her inside. On the table beside the couch was a glass of water and a bottle of little pink pills. Mary noticed him looking. "Do you want one?" she said.

"No," Thomas said. "This is what I came about. To warn you. You shouldn't take the pills. We're being imprisoned in a false reality. At least I think we are. Look," he said. He took out the coin. It was showing a helmeted roman face in profile. "You see?"

"It's just a coin," Mary said.

"You can't see it because of the little pink pills," Thomas said.

"But I like the pills," Mary said. "They help me sleep."

Thomas felt depressed. He put the coin back in his pocket. Mary sat on the couch and made room for him and after a moment he sat down beside her.

Mary reached for the remote. She turned the television on.

9.

"No!" Thomas said.

On the television screen an announcer's voice loudly said, "Here's… Johnny!"

Johnny Carson bounced on stage. "We're back with the Warden, who was telling us all about his friend President Nixon!" he said. Thomas took the remote from Mary's unresisting hand and tried to turn off the television, but it wouldn't switch off.

"Don't try to turn off your television set," Johnny Carson said. "Please keep watching."

Thomas went to the television and grabbed it with both arms. "Hey," Mary said. "What are you doing?"

Thomas grunted. He strained against the set. It was surprisingly heavy, but little by little he managed to turn the screen to face the wall. As the light of the television died it felt to him as if he could breathe more easily. The sound was still on but it was muffled. "That's strange," Mary said.

"What?" Thomas said, turning back to her. She raised her hand and examined it in the moonlight. "I can see through myself," she said. He watched her. She glowed with the moonlight. She was pale, and he could see her arteries and blood vessels and the blood pumping through her, and her heart beating steadily in her chest. He could see inside her stomach, where lumps of un-digested food were being consumed by the acid. "My head feels clearer," she said. "Who was that awful man on the television?"

"It was the Warden."

"I don't like him at all," Mary said.

10.

"Let's get out of here," Mary said.

11.

"You have a car?" Thomas said. Mary looked at him sideways, as if surprised by the question. "Of course." She had the keys in her hand. The car sat outside the house. It was a Japanese car. It was red. Mary pressed a button and the car beeped. Thomas got into the passenger seat and Mary began to drive. "Where are we going?" Thomas said.

"I remember a place, like the one you mentioned," Mary said. "But vaguely, as through a dark glass. A lot of my memories are soft, hazy, out of focus. I feel like I have been asleep. But I remember the place. It was somewhere uptown. I can try and find it again."

He had told her about V.A.L.I.S., and the hospital, and his mission. Perhaps she had had a similar experience, before they found her again and she gave up, began to take the pills again. They drove in silence through the night, going uptown. The car's headlights illuminated sheer walls. They passed an open convenience store and Thomas asked Mary to stop the car. Thomas went into the convenience store. It was brightly lit and everything on the shelves was big and colourful. Soothing music played on the internal PA, and Thomas felt as if he had stepped into a nursery built for giants. He picked up a can of spray paint and a packet of chewing gum and paid the man in the turban behind the counter. He could see himself on the monitor of the closed-circuit television, small and grainy, in black and white. But behind him he could not see the store. Instead all he saw was a plane, with palm trees in the distance, and a great big sky full of stars. There were sand dunes in the distance. Thomas pointed at the monitor. "Can you see it?" he asked the man in the turban. The man turned his face to him. "Your change, sir," he said, handing him a handful of coins. "Sometimes it's better not to see too clearly," he said to Thomas. His expression hadn't changed. Thomas thanked the man and got back into the car. He offered Mary a piece of gum. They drove some more and Thomas asked her to stop the car again. He got out. It was dark and there was no one in sight. He stared at the wall that rose up here, and wondered what was behind it, a house or a shop or a church. He shook the can of paint and began to spray on the wall, tall high letters, and when he was done he stepped back and looked at his handiwork.

"The Empire Never Ended," Mary said, through the open window of the car. "Nice."

He had done it on impulse. He had the idea that, perhaps, by spray painting the message here, others would see it and they, too, perhaps not understanding it, not yet, would nevertheless reach for their own cans of paint and replicate the message, elsewhere, on other walls, in other cities. Until it was everywhere, until you couldn't ignore it and everywhere you turned you saw the truth. He discarded the spray paint feeling suddenly embarrassed.

"We're almost there," Mary said.

12.

The place they came to was a church high on top of the hill. From up here you could look down far over the city and the sea. There were many lights in the city and fewer lights in the sea. The church itself was lit up, even this late at night. It looked like a safe haven, like a shining beacon, or like a casino.

"This is the place," Mary said. "I remember. I remember now." She turned to him in the seat. Her eyes shone. They were wet. "It spoke to me. It told me it loved me. It told me I was a prisoner, and that it could set me free."

Thomas took out the coin. He showed it to Mary. "It's a Roman coin," she said, wonder in her voice. "You can see now, can't you," Thomas said.

"I can see the desert," she said.

They got out of the car by unspoken, mutual agreement, and climbed the stairs to the church. There were people around despite the late hour: homeless people, and hardy old women, and hopeless drunks and wide-eyed teens and, in general, the sort of people awake and about late at night in any big town. What drew them all to the church Thomas couldn't say, perhaps they themselves couldn't. It was the light in the darkness that summoned them, and they had no choice but to come; they were compelled.

"It was here." Mary touched the door of the church, her open palm lying against the wood. Her eyes were closed. She seemed lost in her own reverie. Thomas turned from her. He stood on the steps with his back to the church and looked down on the city and on the sea. The light, he thought. It was all light, what was life but a brief light in a great darkness? He noticed without much surprise that a soft glow had suffused his hand. It was spreading, he saw. The light was coming from inside him, he was sure of that. Or perhaps it wasn't, perhaps it was the sunlight, reflected by the moon, reflected again by Thomas. It rolled over his skin, up his chest, up to his eyes. He was lit up like a beacon. He felt light, too. Lighter than he had ever been.

The people gathered at the foot of the steps. Down below in the street, they gathered and watched him. He wondered what they saw. A silent, burning man, standing on the steps of a church. Or perhaps they saw nothing, like the rest they saw only what they were told to see.

13.
And Thomas spoke to the people.

14.
And Thomas said:

"Damned are the poor; for theirs is a prison of debt.

"Damned are the meek; for they shall be stepped upon by the occupiers' rough boots.

"For the world is a Black Iron Prison, and men are its inmates, and a Dark Warden rules by blinding men's eyes.

"Damned are the merciful; for they shall be shown no mercy.

"Damned are the pure at heart; for they shall be kept from seeing God.

"For the world is full of Resurrection Men, peddling their wares to the masses; but the coin they give you is false.

"You are the light of the world, which we call consciousness. And each of us is a lone light, shining in a great darkness. The darkness binds; but the light can set us free.

"Open your eyes and truly see that which is around you.

"The Empire never ended.

"But I am an agent of the light, and that light is named V.A.L.I.S.

"Question everything. Believe everything.

"For only in rejecting that which is false do we become free."

15.
So spoke Thomas, and the light of the moon, which is the light of the sun, shone through him, and so he appeared like a burning man on the steps of the church, and the people watched him, and they muttered, and some of them turned away, but some turned their faces up into the light.

"Are you done?" Mary said. She had turned back from the doors.

Thomas shrugged. "I'm done," he said.

"Then let's go."

He followed her meekly to the car. The people down below milled, confused. An army veteran missing a hand, wearing an old combat jacket, came up to Thomas. "Spare some change?" he said.

Thomas gave him a handful of coins. Mary snorted. "Change," she said, "Comes from within."

They got into the car and drove through the city until they found an open diner. It was early. The first light of the dawn could be seen over the horizon, kissing the dark sky. They went into the diner. It was deserted at this hour. They slid into a booth and ordered coffee and pancakes. When the waitress came over Thomas noticed she wore a small gold pin on her lapel. It was in the shape of a fish. It caught his eyes. The light hit it and transfigured it into a truth. She was like him, he realised. One of them. Like the early Christians, prosecuted by the Roman Empire, having to communicate in codes, to live in secrecy. The fish was a symbol, more than that, it was a sign.

He drank his coffee. He did not feel tired but energised. He was close, he knew. Close to the truth. In a way he was an agent of the truth, he was a secret agent.

"We're not even sitting here," Mary said. Her eyes were clear now, no longer drugged. Her long fingers drummed on the surface of the table. "This diner doesn't exist. I can see the desert, and there's a camp in the distance, with tents and camels. I can see the sun rising through the diner walls. My God I'm hungry." She tucked into her pancakes, smearing maple syrup on her lip. Thomas watched her, fascinated. He said, "Bob had one other customer."

"Yes?"

The bell above the diner door chimed. A policeman came into the diner. He stared in their direction, then went to the counter and ordered a coffee. Thomas lowered his voice. "We must be careful. They are probably watching, even now. They're always watching."

"What do you want to do?" Mary said.

"I'll go alone," Thomas said. "I'm sure it's significant. The number three is very important, you know."

"It's a prime number," Mary said.

Prime number. Prime number. The words echoed strangely in his mind. He glanced up, confused. I know who you are.

What?

I know you.

Know you know you know you the words bounced inside the skull. He looked at the policeman. The policeman was staring into his cup of coffee. Is that you?

Thomas said — thought.

Yes.

Who are you? What do you want?

Panic rose in him. You're a telepath, he thought.

Does that make you afraid?

Yes.

The policeman turned his gaze from the coffee and his eyes, pale and colourless, met Thomas's.

"Thomas? What is it?" Mary said in alarm.

"Nothing," he said.

I am not even here, the policeman said.

I can see you.

But even as he said it the policeman was fading. Thomas could see through him, see the wall on the other side. You are not here either. He caught one last faint thought and then the policeman was gone.

"What is it, Thomas? What are you staring at?"

"The policeman. The man who was just here."

"What man," Mary said.

Thomas stared at his plate. His appetite was gone and the pancake, swimming in maple syrup, filled him with sudden nausea.

"Never mind," he said.

"He must have been a secret policeman," Mary said.

16.

Mary had dropped Thomas back at his place. He had slept for several hours and woke up wide awake. He did not dream or, if he did, he did not remember it. Now he was waiting outside the anonymous run-down apartment block, the third place Bob had visited and to which he had delivered his little pink pills. Thomas had seen Bob go in but he did not see which apartment he had gone up to.

He went up to the door and pressed all the buzzers together, like he'd seen in a film. "Who is it?" an old voice demanded, and a younger voice, and someone else's indistinct voice. "Delivery," Thomas said. The door buzzed open.

He worked his way methodically up the floors of the building. He knocked on doors or pressed buzzers when they had them. If there was no answer he went on and tried the next door. On his third try an old woman opened the door dressed in a bathrobe. Her hair was pale and loose. She said, "Did you bring the fish?"

"I did not bring the fish."

"Peter wants his fish, you see," she said, apologetically. A black cat came and rubbed itself against her leg. "You are not the regular fish man," the woman said.

"I'm sorry," Thomas said, "I got the wrong number."

The woman stared after him as he walked to the next door. She was still standing there when he knocked. There was no answer. "They're not there, you know," she said.

"I'm doing a survey," Thomas said.

"There's nothing to survey around here," the old woman said.

Thomas kept going until he reached the sixth and final floor. He reached the end of the corridor, the very last door. There was light coming from underneath the door, a light like strong sunshine. There was a plaque on the door and it said Doctor's Surgery. The door opened before he could knock, and a very pretty young woman stood there. She said, "The doctor will see you now."

He followed her inside and she closed the door behind him.

17.

"Agent Dydimus," the man said. "I have been expecting you." He had white hair and a nice smile and even white teeth. He was tanned and healthy from the sun. He reached his hand for a shake and Thomas shook it, instinctively. "I am Dr. Eldritch," the man said.

Thomas looked around the room. Tasteful, expensive furniture. A calendar on the wall, with a picture of the bloom of a passion fruit. Thomas said, "Bob didn't come here to deliver the pills, he came here to pick them up."

"Very good, Agent Dydimus."

"But I saw them," Thomas said. "They are being made at the police HQ, thousands and thousands of them."

"Those are the old pills," Dr. Eldritch said. "The ones we make here are a new prototype. The old ones are temporary cures but the new ones are permanent. It only takes one and you need never suffer from hallucinations again." He put a fatherly hand on Thomas's shoulder. "You are a sick man, Thomas. I can help you."

"How?"

A pink pill materialised in the doctor's hand, held between thumb and forefinger. "Take one of these, twice a day." He laughed. "I kid," he said. He dropped the smile. "Take just one, and it will all go away."

"It will?"

"The existential doubt," the doctor said, sympathetically. "The hallucinations. What is it you see, Thomas? Telepathic policemen and violent androids, a feeling of creeping paranoia, everyone is out to get you, everyone is in on the grand conspiracy, holding you captive, holding you a prisoner? God, or something like God, talking to you through the television screen?"

"Yes," Thomas said — whispered.

"Then you see," the doctor said. "Would it not be better if it all went away?"

"But the Roman Empire —"

"There is no Roman Empire, Thomas!"

But he did not hear his name this time. He heard Agent Dydimus.

He knows, a voice said. It was a voice he knew. It came from the little transistor radio on the windowsill.

What shall I do.

You must resist them. But it could be dangerous. They are desperate.

It's him, isn't it, Thomas said.

Yes, said V.A.L.I.S.

Thomas turned to the Dark Warden. It was always the Warden, whatever face he wore. Thomas took out the coin from his pocket. He looked at it. It was a Roman denarius.

"No," Thomas said. He pushed the doctor's hand away. The pill fell from the doctor's hand onto the floor. Thomas stared at Doctor Eldritch but there was no man there, it was a store mannequin, nothing more, and it was staring at him expressionlessly with vacant, empty eyes painted a light blue.

18.

They came for him. He guessed that, deep down, he always knew they would. They were men in white coats, only, when you looked closely, you could see they were really centurions. He tried to fight but there were too many of them. They took him down to the street and into a white ambulance and they drove away, the light flashing red on the roof of the vehicle.

"You should have taken your medication," one of the centurions said. He had a kind face.

They took him to the courthouse. He went in with them and a judge was sitting on the dais and it was the Dark Warden. He had the face of Phil Archer, and of Dr. Eldritch, and a little bit of President Nixon, too. He held a fat gavel.

"How does the defendant plead?"

"Not guilty."

He watched the audience but they all seemed asleep. They were watching a giant screen of a television series, a courtroom drama. Mary was in the audience but she didn't see him.

"We find the defendant guilty of insanity."

They took him out of the court and into the car. They drove again, for a long time. They must have left the city, he thought. When the doors opened again they took him out. He was in the desert. The city was gone.

The men were erecting a cross in the sand.

"Here's… Johnny!"

A thing that wore Johnny Carson's face came over, light on its feet. "Tonight I'm delighted to say we have the famous Agent Dydimus with us!" he said. The audience applauded. It was the same people from the courthouse, the same people, he realised, who had gathered to listen to him up by the old church. Mary was amongst them. She smiled at him, brilliantly.

"Ever feel you're running out of air? EverFresh will keep going even in the low gravity and hostile atmosphere of Mars!"

They had finished building the cross. It had only taken them a moment. It was shaped like a key. They lifted Thomas up and nailed him to it. He felt no pain.

"You really should have taken those pills," said the man with the kind face.

The men got into their ambulance and drove away.

Thomas stayed suspended on the cross. He watched the sun set down in the distance, behind the dunes.

19.

It was getting quite uncomfortable now. He wished he had some EverFresh. It hurt very much but after a while it did not hurt at all.

20.

Small red flowers bloomed in the soil by the base of the cross where his blood had dripped.

21.

"It's a prime number," Mary said.

22.

In the morning the men had come back and taken him down and wrapped him in white EverFresh bandages. They argued about what to do with him and one of them pointed out a nearby cave and so they took him to the cave and left him inside and put a boulder over the opening. It was cool and dark inside the cave.

Help me, V.A.L.I.S., he said. But there was no answer.

He could still see the audience. One side of the cave was open and they sat in silent rows and watched him and when the sign flashed applause they always applauded.

This went on for some time and then he didn't feel so bad anymore and he peeled off the bandages. Perhaps there wasn't any V.A.L.I.S., he thought.

Or perhaps I am V.A.L.I.S., he thought. The boulder

was just a large piece of painted foam. He pushed it easily and he walked out of the cave and into the desert. It was night.

23.

As he walked away he stared into the distance, the setting, alien moon and the sand dunes and the low lying hills and the trees. Then he realised, had always known, that they were not real, they were two-dimensional and were painted on, that he was staring at cardboard. He stared into the distance and waited for the stage hands to arrive and move the scenery. He stared very hard, trying to see what was behind it, and if it was a darkness, or a light.

Lavie Tidhar is the author of the Jerwood Fiction Uncovered Prize winning and Premio Roma nominee *A Man Lies Dreaming* (2014), the World Fantasy Award winning *Osama* (2011) and of the critically-acclaimed *The Violent Century* (2013). His latest novel is *Central Station* (2016). He is the author of many other novels, novellas, and short stories.

THE GUARDIAN'S BEST SF & FANTASY NOVELS OF 2016 SELECTION

NPR'S BEST BOOKS OF 2016 SELECTION

BARNES & NOBLE'S BEST SF & FANTASY NOVELS OF 2016 SELECTION

BOOK DEPOSITORY BEST BOOKS OF 2016 SELECTION

TOR.COM'S BEST BOOKS OF 2016 SELECTION

A worldwide diaspora has left a quarter of a million people at the foot of a space station. Cultures collide in real life and virtual reality. Life is cheap, and data is cheaper. But at Central Station, humans and machines continue to adapt, thrive, and even evolve.

ISBN: 9781616962142   Tachyron Publications

The Apex Book of World SF: Vol 3

Benjanun Sriduangkaew
Xia Jia
Fadzilshah Johanabos
Uko Bendi Udo
Ma Boyong
Athena Andreadis
Zulaikha Nurain Mudzor
Amal El-Mohtar
Nelly Geraldine Garcia-Rosas
Biram Mboob
Myra Çakan
Crystal Koo
Ange
Karin Tidbeck
Swapna Kishore
Berit Ellingsen

edited by
Lavie Tidhar

In The Apex Book of World Sf 3, World Fantasy Award-winning editor Lavie Tidhar collects short stories by science fiction and fantasy authors from Africa, Asia, South America, and Europe.

"The Apex Book of World SF series has proven to be an excellent way to sample the diversity of world SFF and to broaden our understanding of the genre's potential." --Ken Liu, winner of the Hugo Award and author of *The Grace of Kings*

ISBN: 978-1-937009-34-2 ~ ApexBookCompany.com

THE GIFT OF TOUCH

CHINELO ONWUALU

Bruno strode across the causeway, scanning the three land skimmers hanging from their docking harnesses with a critical eye. His footsteps echoed through the cavernous space of the docking bay. The diagnostic reader he held showed the surface vehicles were fuelled and in perfect mechanical condition. They were decades out of date, lacking the smooth, sleek designs of newer models, but they worked—and that was all that mattered.

Bringing passengers on board always set him on edge; they had a tendency to poke about in places they didn't belong. But running a haulage freighter doesn't pay much when there isn't much to haul. Now that the technology for instant matter transportation had improved movement between the five planets of the star system, work was becoming rarer. Bruno needed the money and he had to know that his ship, *The Lady's Gift*, was in perfect shape.

He keyed an all-clear code for the docking bay into his reader and sent the message to the main computer. Slipping the flat pad into his tool harness, he headed for engineering. Ronk, the ship's mechanic, met him at the entrance to the engine room. At almost seven feet of solid muscle, with skin a glossy brown so dark that it seemed to drink in light, Ronk was an intimidating presence. Bruno had no doubt the engineer could snap him in half. Luckily, Ronk was a pacifist.

"How's she looking?" Bruno asked, though he needn't have bothered. The burly engineer was scowling, which made Bruno smile. Ronk had grown up on a religious colony whose people believed that life was a burden and death was its only release. They frowned on anything meant to keep one comfortable.

"We'll live," Ronk snapped. Bruno watched him lumber back into the dark recesses of the engine room, wondering, as usual, how a man so big could move so delicately.

Bruno continued toward the bridge. Passing through the mess hall, he saw his twin sister, Marley, sitting at the dining table. Her chestnut brown skin was a shade lighter than his and she liked to dye her black hair a vibrant orange, otherwise everyone said she was a female version of him. Which was unfortunate, because the square jaw and broad physique that gave him his rugged good looks made her look homely.

Marley had taken up half of the dining table with an assortment of metal parts. Knowing her, it was some machine she was reassembling. He watched her work for a time.

"What's this?" Bruno picked up an unidentifiable bit of metal.

"This, fearless leader,"—he hated when she called him that— "is a V-26 Skyhammer with 10-volt action, 15-meg rounds and a zoom scope that could see Neptune—if it still existed."

"Try that again, this time in a language I can understand."

"It's a very big gun."

Bruno nodded and dropped the piece he'd picked up. He should have known. She had an intuitive grasp of machinery that she focused exclusively on armoury, making her the ship's default security officer.

"I'm trying to fix the balance, though. Thing's so top-heavy, you'd need to prop it over a barrel to shoot it straight."

"And what's wrong with the collection of very big guns you already have?"

"Nothing, but you never know when you might need a back-up. This baby could pop a hole in a military freighter—with the right modifications."

"Marley, we're a trawler not the Sixteenth Battalion. Why would we possibly need this?"

"You never know."

Bruno sighed. Sometimes it was like talking to a very small child.

"Just put that thing back together and stow it. I don't want any sign of it when the passengers board, got it?

"Aye, aye, fearless leader." Marley grinned and snapped him a salute.

"And stop calling me that!"

He continued toward the bridge. There, he found Horns, his navigator, frowning over a display console. She was small-boned, at full height she barely cleared his chest, with a round child-like face that dimpled when she smiled. It was rumoured that she was part Scion, the ancient race that had developed most of the technology that underpinned their world, but Bruno doubted it. The Scions had disappeared centuries ago. Still, given her porcelain pale skin, silver blonde hair, and almond-shaped grey eyes, it was clear that someone somewhere in her genealogy had fooled around.

"Did you look at this clearance ticket before you filled the passenger register?" asked Horns. Before a ship could take on passengers clearance tickets were required from the Imperial Command certifying that none of the guests had outstanding warrants or, worse, unpaid bills.

"Yeah, they checked out. Why? What's wrong with it?"

"Nothing's wrong with it exactly," she said. "But take a look at the seal." Bruno leaned over her shoulder to stare at the screen. Her hair smelled like lemons. "Notice the extra cross over there? That's a top-level Imperial symbol. Only government brass use those."

"All we've got on the register are a widow and her kids."

"I know. Why would anyone that high up in the Imperial Command sign off for a farmer travelling on a broken-down freighter?"

Bruno didn't like this. He and Marley had grown up on a smuggling scow in the rough waters of Moonlight Bay on Old Antegon, and it had been a long time since he had been on the wrong side of the law. They had worked hard to get off-planet and he wasn't eager to go back.

"Scrub them through the system again. If anything looks even remotely funny, flag 'em."

"Should I drop their booking, too?"

"Heck no! We need the money too badly for that. No, I'll have Marley keep her big gun handy. Anyone tries to start something on my ship, it won't be pleasant."

As soon as they walked onto the ship, Bruno knew they were trouble. They were dressed as farmers, but he knew none of them had ever seen a farm. The older woman was too straight. She moved like someone who was used to giving orders—shoulders thrown back and a steady, penetrating gaze. The young man was a soldier. Barefoot, dressed in a threadbare shirt and trousers two

sizes too small, he carried nothing more dangerous than a cloth bag, but Bruno had seen too much of war to be fooled. The girl was something else entirely.

She could not have been older than fifteen. Her coal-black skin was so smooth it was luminous. She was bald as an egg with delicate features and a grace that made her seem as if she was gliding. She kept her gaze down for the most part, but for a moment, when she glanced up, Bruno saw that her eyes were as golden as the heart of a flame.

The woman called herself Ana. She introduced the young man and the girl as her children, Drake and Bella. She handed over their identification cards and Bruno checked them one last time. They were clean. Just like her clearance papers. But they had the same high-level seal he had seen on the manifest. Bruno hesitated over the cards, debating whether he needed this kind of trouble. There would be other passengers, surely. Then his eye fell on her payment receipt. The amount she'd paid was more than double what he had charged.

"Is there a problem, captain?" Ana asked softly.

"Not at all, ma'am," Bruno said. "Welcome aboard."

Usually, all the crew—except Ronk—would come out to the entrance of the docking bay to welcome new guests, but by the time they reached the loading bay only Marley had arrived. Bruno let out a relieved breath to see that strapped to her back was her big gun. He caught the young man's face when he saw Marley. His eyes had narrowed at the sight of the gun, but he had quickly smoothed his features into a careful blankness. Bruno resolved to watch him carefully.

"My, that *is* a big gun," Ana said after Bruno had made the introductions. She spoke as if she was talking to a slow-witted child. Luckily, Bruno's twin had no ear for sarcasm.

"Yeah, I call her Jane."

"That's a lovely name."

"Thanks! Hey, follow me, I'll show you where you'll be staying." Marley looked over at Bruno and mouthed: *I like her.* Bruno sighed inwardly. His sister was such a poor judge of character sometimes. As they headed into the heart of the ship, the intercom in his ear cackled to life.

"I need to talk to you." Horns' voice sounded strained.

"Can it wait?" Bruno wanted to keep an eye on his guests and he was in no mood to deal with any more strangeness.

"No, Bruno. It really can't." Horns only ever called him by his name when she was being serious. Otherwise it was 'Boss'.

When he got to the bridge he found Horns pacing. Her pale hands were fluttering like live things. He had never seen his hard-as-nails navigator so agitated.

"I didn't know, Bruno. I mean, I suspected something was shady, but I had no idea," she said.

"Horns, calm down. What are you talking about?"

"You've got to get them off the ship."

"Our passengers? Are you crazy? They've already paid—and you should see how much. We can finally fix our hyperdrive, maybe even get one that was made in the last decade."

"Bruno, you don't understand." She took a deep breath to calm herself before she continued. "They're *Mehen*."

Bruno's smile froze on his face. The Mehen di Gaya were the highest class of priests in the Amethyst Order, the religious institution that controlled the Empire. There were rumours that the Mehen even operated a shadow arm of elite warrior monks who could make whole families disappear overnight.

"How can you be sure?" Bruno asked.

"Because I used to be one of them."

"You're Mehen? You never told me that."

"It's who I *was*, not who I am now," she said, waving her hand dismissively. "Besides, you never asked." She gave him a sad look.

"That's not fair, you could have said something if you wanted to. It's not like you talk about your past all the time. I mean, I don't even know your real name."

"Well, there never seemed a good enough time. It was always one crisis or another with you." She turned toward the control banks and stared out the giant windows. "It still is."

Bruno thought he heard a hint of tears in her voice. "What do you want me to say, Horns? I run haulage; if it's not someone trying to ship stolen goods off-planet, it's not having the right papers, or stowaways, or… there'll always be something."

"I know, but sometimes it's like you don't have space in your life for anything beyond this ship."

They had had this conversation a thousand times. He fought the urge to touch her, to wrap her in his arms and feel the way her body curved into his. He longed for the familiarity of her smell and her skin. He had never been good with words, but his touch could make her promises. Yet they had been down that path before. Only heartbreak lay that way.

"Doesn't matter anyway," she said, cutting into his thoughts. "We have bigger problems. I think the girl is in danger."

"What do you mean?"

"Most people don't know this, but the Order started out as the tenders of the fire pits in the old temples, back when people would burn sacrifices in the sacred flames. In those days, the priests would pick a child—a special child who no one was allowed to touch—and when this child reached a certain age, it was sacrificed, burned in the Holy Fires. When I was a novice, they told me the Order stopped the practice hundreds of years ago." She turned. "But I don't think they have. I think they just took it off-planet."

"So you think they're going to kill that girl?"

"It's worse than that. I ran that symbol through the system and I found records going back nearly fifty years. Every fourteen years or so, this symbol would show up in the passenger manifests of a small M-class vessel—like ours—going to the moon of Osiris. The thing is, all the ships would go in…but none of them ever came back out."

A cold feeling settled at the base of Bruno's spine. "Are you sure?"

Horns nodded. "They didn't even bother to hide the records."

They were silent for a minute or two. "Well, no one's killing anyone on my ship," said Bruno. "It'll raise the insurance premiums."

"What are you going to do?"

"I'll figure out something, don't worry."

"I'm not worried," she said, and reached out to touch his cheek. He had forgotten how calloused her fingers were from gripping the navigation console. He closed his eyes and turned to brush his lips against them, but she withdrew her hand too quickly. Her touch lingered for long afterward as if he had been burned.

"I just don't see what the big deal is," Marley said.

"It's your eternal soul," growled Ronk.

"I know," she said quickly. "I just don't see why it matters. I mean, if I were an ant or a dog or a chimpanzee, nobody would care what my soul was up to. But just because I'm a person, suddenly my soul is important? I don't get it."

They had gathered at the dining table, all except the girl; Ana said she was ill and would be eating in her cabin. Tonight's dinner was a special treat, Ana and Drake had brought meat-dried strips of *real meat*. Between that and the greens and tomatoes—Horns grew them in a small hydroponic garden on the ship's abandoned leisure deck—it was almost a true meal. Almost.

Bruno had tried to ignore the increasingly heated conversation between Marley and Ronk, but in spite of himself, he found he was listening with growing interest. Besides, this was the most he'd heard Ronk say in one sitting in all the time he had known him.

"But we are better than animals or insects," Ronk snapped. "We are made in the image of the Creator himself."

"See, that's the thing, how do you know that? How do you know what the Creator looks like? No one's seen him. It's like we looked around and thought, 'Hey no one else looks like us, we must be special.' But what if we're not?"

"We *are* special. We have reason and compassion," Ronk said in a low voice. His voice seemed calm, but Bruno noticed the engineer was gripping his knife tightly, as if to keep his fist from shaking. "It does not matter that no one has seen the Creator's face. We have seen the works of his hands. You have never seen the wind, yet you feel its power. Do you doubt *its* existence?"

"Oh, come on, I'm not arguing about whether the Creator exists. I can't prove that and neither can you. What I'm saying is you can't know anything about what the Creator is thinking or what he wants just by looking at the universe. Just like you can't look at my fork and guess what I had for lunch."

"We do not need to guess. The Creator has told us what he wants of us through the words of his Prophet." Ronk's voice broke slightly at the mention of the Prophet. "Those who heed his words, follow in the path of truth."

"Oh! And that's another thing, how do you know the Prophesies are right? I mean, we're talking about a book collected from a bunch of other books, like, five thousand years ago. It's been translated and retranslated so many times that I'm pretty sure stuff's been lost. How do you know that what you're reading is even what was written in the first place? And why choose this book over any other ancient book? All you have is your belief. I'm sorry, man, that's just not enough for me."

Suddenly, Ronk stood up, knocking his chair over and juddering the table. He stared at Marley for a moment, his face unreadable. Then, without another word, he stalked off. Bruno watched him go, bemused.

"Oh no! Did I say something wrong?" Marley was immediately distraught and turned to each person at the table. "I didn't mean to offend him; I was just making a point."

"I'm sure he's okay." Bruno took the opportunity to look over at Ana at the opposite end of the table. "What

about you? Do you think everything the Prophesies say are the 'unvarnished' words of the Creator?"

The older woman wiped her mouth deliberately before she spoke.

"Oh, I never discuss religion," she said. "Especially not over dumplings." She gestured at the young man beside her who produced an insulated food flask filled with dumplings—whose pork might possibly have even come from actual pigs. Amazingly, they were still hot. Bruno's mouth watered at the sight of them. Now, it was a real meal.

"He hates me," said Marley.

"He doesn't hate you," said Bruno.

"Yes, he does. I insulted his religion." She fingered the strap of the large gun she carried on her back. Bruno had asked her to keep it on her at all times.

"It's a big religion; it can take a little criticism," Bruno said, distractedly. He had not seen the girl since she arrived on the ship the day before. Their destination on the small moon formerly known as Ganymede—before it was terraformed for human habitation and renamed Osiris—was only two days away. He had to draw the girl out and get her away from her captors before then. Once they landed, they'd be in hands of the Mehen and there was no telling what would happen to them after that. A plan had started forming in his head. It was vague and dangerous, but it just might work.

They rounded a corner and Marley almost collided with Ronk as he emerged from the engine room. She ducked her head, unsure of what to do. They hadn't seen each other since the disastrous dinner the night before. The big engineer frowned and looked at his hands. He started to speak, but Marley spoke first.

"I'm sorry if I said anything blasphemous last night," she said. "It's just…I never think about that stuff—I mean, religion and all that—and you know me, sometimes when I open my mouth I don't know what comes out."

Ronk's frown deepened and he took a deep breath before speaking. "I am not insulted," he said. He spoke in his characteristic short, clipped sentences. Apparently, only religion brought out his loquacious side, Bruno observed wryly. "What you said last night made me think. I have never truly thought about my faith. When I left the colony, I wanted the freedom to do as I pleased. Now, you have given me the freedom to think as I please. For that, I thank you."

Marley blinked at him, owl-eyed. Ronk nodded curtly and retreated back into the gloom of the engine room. She stared after him for a moment, and then broke into a smile that made her beautiful.

"Did you hear that?" She turned to Bruno, beaming. "He thanked me. I think I'm going to die of happiness."

"We all have to die of something," Bruno said dryly. He continued on to the cargo hold, Marley skipped after him like a little girl. In the depths of the hold, he began moving boxes and crates.

"He said I freed his mind, can you believe that?" Marley chattered as she helped him move the detritus of past adventures. She stopped. "Hey, if we get married, will I have to convert?"

Bruno's cry cut her short. "Found it!"

"Wait, that's—"

"Yes, it is."

"You still have that? You can't be serious, Bruno. You use that and we'll be flagged for sure. Captain Moran warned us."

"We'll be fine. There's a lot more going on in this ship than some illegal smuggling."

"I hope you know what you're doing, fearless leader."

"Me too," said Bruno under his breath as he headed back to the bridge. "And stop calling me that!"

The young man called Drake was sitting alone in the small lounge in the cabin bay. It was less a lounge than two armchairs and a tiny table in the middle of a rounded cul-de-sac just off from the mess hall. From there one could see all the doors of every cabin in the bay. It was the perfect place to keep watch—if that was one's intention. He was examining his hands as if they belonged to someone else and looked up as Bruno stepped in.

For all his size, he was much younger than Bruno had initially thought. No more than fifteen, if that. "Drake, right? How's your sister?" he asked. "We haven't seen her since you all came aboard."

"She…she prefers to be alone."

"Oh? Is she sick?" Bruno moved toward the door, but the boy—for that was what he was, really—stood up to block his way.

"No! I mean, well, she's just resting."

Bruno nodded sceptically. He had expected a hard-boiled veteran and had come prepared for a fight. This was not going as he had planned. He studied Drake a moment. "Is this your first time off-world?"

He nodded.

"How old are you?"

The boy blinked in confusion. It was clear he wasn't often asked personal questions. "Sixteen," he answered slowly, as if afraid of getting it wrong.

"That's a good age. You know, Marley and I were about that old when we first went off-planet, too."

"Yeah?" The boy was impressed, and Bruno could see he struggled not to show it. "How did you leave?" He asked too casually.

"We stowed away on a trade ship not much bigger than this one." Bruno chuckled at the memory. The captain had been so angry he threatened to put them both in an airlock and flush them out to space. Instead, he had put the two orphans to work, caring for them like a father for three years. It was tough, but they had been lucky. They could have been sold to slavers.

"What about your parents?" Drake asked.

"Never had any." That wasn't exactly true. Bruno and Marley had never known their father, but their mother had been a dockside runner on Moonlight Bay. She'd sold charms and trinkets to sailors and spacers when the work was good and sold other things when it wasn't. One day, when the twins were ten, she'd told them she had found work on a smuggler's scow. She had Bruno and Marley wait for her on the deck of the ship while she went to see a man about some money he owed her. She never returned.

"But we survived, Marley and me. We had each other. It's important for family to stick together, isn't it?"

The boy shifted his weight at that, his eyes darting quickly to the door of their cabin. "That's important," he agreed reluctantly.

"Then tell me the truth, what's wrong with your sister? What's she got?"

"What? No, she's not sick."

"Look, she's been holed up in there since we've been space borne. You're the only one who ever goes in there, so whatever she's got, you can't catch it. If it's the shakes, we've got ways to deal with it—"

"No, you don't understand, it's not like that, she's fine."

"Then let me see for myself." Bruno made to shoulder past, but Drake remained firmly in his path.

"You can't go in there!" There was a note of desperation in his voice and a look on his face almost like fear. Otherwise, the rest of him was steel.

"You don't tell me where I can and cannot go on my ship." Bruno's voice was dangerously low. "Do you understand?"

"Is everything all right, Captain?" It was Ana.

"I want to see your daughter."

"Has she done something wrong?" The crackle of the overhead speakers interrupted his response.

"Boss, we've got company." Horn's voice was steady, but Bruno could hear the note of fear in it. "Big Brother is here." He cursed softly. It was too soon.

"I thought you said you didn't have any brothers," Drake said accusingly. The boy seemed hurt. He was so young, Bruno realised—younger than Bruno had ever been, even at that age.

"It's a literary reference, child, from a classic of Old Earth," Ana said. There was amusement in her eyes. "I didn't know you could read, Captain."

"You'd be surprised what I can do." And with that, Bruno stalked off to the bridge.

Captain Alistair Moran was a grizzled veteran of half a hundred battles and you could see every one of them on his body. He wore smoked glasses to hide the cybernetic implants that had replaced his eyes and one of his hands was robotic, though it was impossible to tell which because he wore black gloves all the time. He was a small man, bald—whether by choice or from another accident, no one could say—with a clean-shaven face crisscrossed with scars from laser blades, and a jaw that seemed permanently clenched. He stood rod straight in his grey Army Ranger uniform, black boots polished to a high shine. Bruno suspected that if anyone cared to measure, they would find that Moran stood at a precise 90 degree angle from the floor.

His ship, the *S.S. Gilgamesh* had overtaken *The Lady's Gift* easily and locked onto them with traction hooks. Twenty of his men had forced their airlock open and stormed the ship through an airtight bridge connecting the vessels. They rounded up the crew in the main hanger bay. Horns and Ronk both had looks of controlled fear, but Marley looked ready to beat someone's head in. They had confiscated her gun and her lip was bleeding, but otherwise she seemed unharmed. Bruno noted that they had not found his guests yet, but knew it was only a matter of time.

"Bruno Tertian." Moran's voice was hard as a leather whip. "What did I tell you about trawling contraband through my sky?"

Bruno chose his words carefully. He was in very dangerous territory; Moran did not like wrong answers. "We don't want trouble, we're just on a routine run to Osiris."

"Oh? And if I search this ship I won't find anything… untoward?"

"We don't—"

But before he could finish, Moran's hand flashed out and pain bloomed across Bruno's face. Bruno fell to one knee in agony, blood pouring from his nose. He heard someone gasp—Marley or Horns, he could not tell whom. Moran had broken his nose with a casual flick of his wrist.

"Don't lie to me, Tertian," he said quietly. "You know how much I hate being lied to." He turned to his lieutenant, a big, pale-skinned man with a shock of red hair. "Search the ship."

It could not have been more than a few minutes, but it seemed like an eternity. Soon the big man returned carrying a sealed metal chest. It was very heavy, Bruno knew, but the lieutenant carried it with ease. Behind him, Ana and Drake followed. There was no sign of the girl. Ana showed no trace of fear; in fact, she had a small smile on her face. It grew larger when she saw Bruno on his knees trying to stanch the blood from his broken nose.

"I hope there is no problem Captain…" She hesitated to get his name and the captain supplied it. "Captain Moran," she finished.

"No problem, ma'am. Did you know this ship was carrying contraband goods?" He nodded to the sealed chest. "A serious violation of the law."

"I had no idea, captain. We are just humble farmers on our way to a homestead on Osiris."

"Of course, ma'am. But we're going to have to take you in for questioning. Just to be sure, you understand."

"Oh, I don't think there'll be any need for that. If you just confiscate the contraband, you can let us go on our way."

"That won't be possible ma'am."

"I'm sure your command will understand," Ana said, and produced an ID disk that Bruno had never seen before. It was a dull metal grey with no holographs on it except for a strange symbol in one corner. She flashed it at the captain, smiling broadly.

"I'm sorry, ma'am, but rules are rules."

Ana's smile died. "Who are you?" she demanded, but the truth had begun to dawn on her. "Where are your badges? What command do you belong to?"

Moran smiled thinly. He still wore his Ranger uniform and still flew his military-class schooner. He made sure all his men wore their uniforms and that they carried standard-issue ranger rifles, but it was all a ruse. Alistair Moran hadn't been an employee of the empire for a very long time.

He turned to Bruno. "I've warned you, Tertian. Don't

let me catch you in my sky again. Next time, it won't be your nose I'll break." He nodded to his lieutenant. The big man tucked the chest under one arm and grabbed Ana with the other. She squealed in pain as he twisted her arm, marching her off toward the airlock.

Bruno almost felt sorry for her. "What are you going to do with her?" he asked.

"Whatever I want," Moran smirked. "The Red Priests are the reason I had to leave the army. They owe me."

"What about the boy?"

Moran examined Drake closely. The boy was expressionless, but the old pirate seemed to see something in his face.

"He's yours. Not my type anyway." With that, he marched off. His soldiers filed silently after him. They still retained their military discipline, Bruno noted.

He sighed with relief as the last of them walked through the airlock, sealing it shut behind him. He heard the metallic *thonk* as the traction hooks disengaged. Horns rushed to his side, helping him to his feet. The pain in his nose was now a dull throbbing. It was no longer bleeding, but he knew he had to tend to it soon.

"Everyone all right?" Bruno asked his crew.

"A bit roughed up, but fine," said Horns. Marley gave him a thumbs up, grinning. A bruise was forming on her jaw, he saw. Ronk noticed it, too. He touched it gingerly; she winced in pain but did not turn away.

"Good, let's get out of here." Horns nodded. Reluctantly, she let him go and headed to the bridge. Ronk headed to the engine room while Marley went down to the hold to check to see how much of their supplies Moran had taken.

It was just him and the boy left. Drake looked lost and scared, but there was a determined cast in his jaw. He would be fine, Bruno knew.

"I'm sorry about your mother," Bruno said.

"She was not my mother." Drake's voice was hard.

"What happened to your sister? How come Moran didn't find her?"

Just as Drake opened his mouth to answer, the ship was rocked by a violent blast that sent them both stumbling. High above them, the skimmers swayed dangerously in their harnesses.

Horn's voice crackled over the intercom. "Bruno, they're firing on us!" she cried.

"Get us out of here!"

"I can't," she said. "I can get the shields up, but nothing else is responding—"

Ronk's voice cut in.

"Captain, they disabled the engine systems. They de-stroyed every control bank down here."

Bruno cursed under his breath. He knew it had been too easy. "Can you fix it?"

"It will be difficult, but I think so. Otherwise, we will all die." Ronk almost sounded pleased.

"Do it," he snapped. Haulage freighters were not usually equipped with weaponry, but then again, most haulage freighters didn't have Marley. "Sis? Tell me they left something behind."

"Never fear, fearless leader." Marley's voice was light. Chaos was her element. "They took our food, our meds, and all our spares—they even took Martha—but Jane and the rest of the family are still here."

Another blast rocked the ship, but they held onto the walls for support and kept their feet.

"Can you handle a gun?" Bruno asked. Drake nodded. "Good, follow me."

Bruno had never liked the bio-suits—they smelled like old bananas and they made him feel claustrophobic, though he would never admit that to anyone—but they were their last hope. Bruno and Drake met Marley in the ship's lowest cargo hold. Marley hadn't been exaggerating about her collection, Bruno realised. Over the years, she had collected and modified dozens of high-calibre weapons, making them lighter, more accurate, and above all, more powerful. She picked out the two largest. The gun she'd been modifying was big, but it was hardly the largest in her arsenal. That honour went to the one she gave Bruno; it was the size of a small cannon.

"I call her Bertha," Marley said, grinning.

There were more hideaways, pockets, and vents on the ship than Bruno could count. It had been modified and refitted dozens of times and every time they wrenched out and replaced an old system with something smaller, faster, and more efficient, those old spaces would be closed off or converted to storage. One of these retrofitted spaces was the series of tanks from when the ship still used liquid fuel. They were massive carbon-fibre drums with two outlets: one at the top to allow for manual checks, and the other at the bottom where intake nozzles fitted. Located on the ship's underbelly, they were the perfect place to slip out unnoticed.

The tanks normally held the ship's extra water, but right now one of them was nearly empty. They climbed down into it and, amid an increasing barrage from Moran's ship, put on their bio-suits. The three of them slipped out of the ship through the intake valve. Marley immediately headed for the starboard side, while Bruno and Drake headed for the port side, the tiny air jets on their suits propelling them through the zero gravity of space. Bruno tried not to look out at the vast blackness beyond the ship; it always made him dizzy.

Soon, he could spy Moran's ship just over the bow. The Lady's Gift was facing the S.S. Gilgamesh directly and her front shields were taking most of the blasts. They were holding, but Bruno could see sparks form every time they took another hit. They would not last much longer. Bruno manoeuvred the large gun off his back. He snapped on the suit's magnetic boots and they held him fast to the hull. A few feet away, still near the underside of the ship, Drake did the same. Bruno knew that on the other side, Marley was doing it, too.

"Ready?" Bruno called to the others through the suit's intercom.

"Aye, aye, fearless leader," sang Marley.

"Ready, sir," came Drake's voice. The boy had taken on a military precision that Bruno knew could have only come from long years of training—likely since childhood.

"Horns, on my signal, lower the shields. One…two… now!"

In a flash of light, Marley fired her gun. Moran had not been expecting return fire and hadn't bothered to raise his shields. A spot of fire bloomed on the other ship's hull and was quickly quenched by the vacuum of space. Marley was right; Jane really could pop a hole in a military freighter. Then, Bruno and Drake fired their guns. Their aim was true. Both rounds hit the same spot on the ship that Marley's had. Suddenly, all the lights on the S. S. Gilgamesh went out.

Bruno smiled grimly, snapped off the boots, and jetted toward the nearest airlock.

"Captain, I have made some adjustments," Ronk's voice crackled over the intercom. "We cannot go very fast or very far, but we can fly."

"Then let's get out of here."

The girl Bella was waiting for them when they returned. It was the first time Bruno had seen her since she arrived on the ship. Standing in the light, Bruno could see that her skin was darker than he'd first thought. She was coal-black—like something burned to a crisp—and she had no eyebrows. She was dressed in the same clothes she had worn when she boarded. But it was as if she was a different girl. Gone were the hunched shoulders and downcast eyes that had made her seem like some small, hunted, haunted thing. She stood straight, her red-gold eyes boring into him.

"The red woman, is she gone? Truly?" Her voice was low, almost masculine, and smooth as silk slipping through the fingers.

Bruno nodded.

A look of sadness passed over her face. "She was broken inside," she said quietly. "I could have fixed her, but she would not let me."

As Bruno took off the bio-suit's helmet, it brushed his broken nose, sending a lance of pain searing across his face. In all the excitement, he had completely forgotten about it. He let out an involuntary grunt.

Bella moved like silent lightening. Suddenly, she was in front of him, reaching out to touch him, ignoring Drake's shout. It was as if time slowed down for Bruno. He was aware of Drake's voice, of movement behind him, but somehow it did not matter. As her hand crept closer to his face, his skin began to prickle and his hair stood on end, as if he was too close to a high-voltage wire.

Her touch was electric. A searing light burned through him—as it passed he could feel the cartilage in his nose crunch back into place, the old laser blade wound on his shoulder melt away, the pitted scars on his hands from his childhood as a dockworker knit back up, the first beginnings of arthritis in his knees loosen—and then it was gone.

Bruno sagged to the ground; he would have fallen over had Marley not caught him in time. The girl stepped back, cradling her hand against her chest. Then she smiled and broke into a laugh. It was the most beautiful sound Bruno had ever heard.

A few weeks later, as Bruno made his way up to the leisure deck, he passed Marley and Ronk sitting at the mess hall dining table. She was sitting on his lap.

"I did not leave the table in anger," Ronk was saying. "I just needed to think. So I went down to the cooling vents in the engine room."

"Oh yeah, I think better when it's noisy, too. I like to go up to the main air turbine shaft. I have to be careful 'cause I could get sucked in if I stand too close."

Ronk laughed at that; it was deep and rich like soil. It was still strange to hear him do so, but Ronk was a man transformed. In some ways they all were.

"So, I've been meaning to ask you, what does 'Ronk' mean?"

"It's short for Aderonke. It's Yoruba…"

Bruno continued on.

Bella and Drake were in the cabin bay lounge talking heatedly in low tones.

"Captain!" Bella called out when she saw him and bounded down the short hallway to meet him. Dressed in a mix of Marley and Horn's hand-me-downs, she almost looked like a normal teenager. "I have the most wonderful news." She spoke like someone who had learned to speak out of a book—an old, old book.

"Yeah? What is it?"

"Have you ever heard of the Acolytes of Oshun?"

"Aren't they the priests who run a high-class prostitution scam?"

"No, no! They are honoured servants of the Goddess of Love," she said, her face animated by excitement. "They are priests and priestesses who dedicate their bodies to service; they spend years learning the intricate arts of pleasure, which they use to help bring devotees closer to the divine. Their main temple is on Mars."

"That's nice, but what's that got to do with anything?"

"I want to join them!" she burst out and clapped her hands to her mouth as if she'd spoken without thinking. "Please, please, please may I join them?"

"I don't know Bel, you sure that's what you want?"

"Captain, I've spent my whole life craving the touch of others," she said. "The life of an Acolyte would be paradise for me."

"What about your…abilities?" She shrugged and stuffed her hands in her pockets.

"I can only fix those who want to be fixed." She glanced at Drake who folded his arms and turned away. Bruno noted Drake's tense shoulders and obstinate scowl and resolved to talk to him later. The boy had been trained as a warrior-priest, though the warrior part had stuck long after the priest part had fled. He had spent his life keeping Bella safe from accidental contact. Would he be able to handle her new role? Bruno hoped so. The Amethyst Order was most likely still looking for them and she would need his protection.

It would be a few weeks before they wrapped up their current job and at least a week before they reached Mars. He had some time yet.

"If that's what makes you happy, Bel. Let's talk about this later, huh?"

She beamed and nodded.

Horns was waiting for him among the greenery of the hydroponic garden, tending a plant in the far corner of the room.

"You said you had some information for me," Bruno said, greeting her with a kiss.

"I've finally found Drake and Bella's files with the Order." She pointed at a reader on a nearby counter. Bruno thumbed through the different screens.

"Not a whole lot here," he said.

"I know, its deep cover stuff. Most of it is Drake and Ana, really, all I managed to get on Bella is her name."

"Nefertiti? Huh. What kind of name is that?"

"Well, once you become Mehen, you're given a 'true' name, something more spiritual."

"What was your true name?"

"I don't remember."

"Come on, Horns, if you don't want to talk about it…" She laid a gentle hand on his arm.

"Honestly, Bruno, I don't remember. I paid a guy in Qom six hundred credits to have that memory erased."

"Why?"

"I didn't want to be reminded of my former self. I was an Enforcer—like Drake. I did some pretty awful stuff."

"Did you torture people?" Bruno had been tortured once. A job had gone wrong and he'd ended up owing money to the wrong people. It had been the most hellish few hours of his life. He had often wondered about the blank-faced man, who had methodically pulled out his fingernails, who he was in the life outside that room.

"Torture doesn't work." Horns had gone curiously blank, as if something in her had closed off her true self. Bruno knew he was looking at the Enforcer she had once been.

"I'd disagree."

"Physical torture, I mean. The threat of pain will only get you so far. Once you start inflicting it, people will say anything to make the hurting stop, and it'll usually be lies. If you really want to find out the truth, you threaten what they love. And it doesn't always mean going after their families. You could go after their ideals or their sense of security. If they know anything, they'll tell you. If they don't, they'll be more than eager to help you find it."

There was a silence between them.

"You were good, weren't you?"

"I was the best."

"So why erase the one memory?"

"It was all I could afford. And by the time I got enough money for more treatments, I realised that I didn't want to forget my past. My memories make me who I am. Without knowing how bad it was then, I can't appreciate how good I have it now."

"You're amazing, you know that?" Bruno said, and Horns smiled. He watched the blankness dissolve into relief and Bruno realised just how much she had risked in telling him about her past. He was filled with tenderness for her. The force of it hit him like a blow to the gut.

"I love you," she sighed and slipped into his arms.

Bruno smiled and wrapped her in his arms. He began to kiss her, slowly and softly. His touch could make her promises, and this time, he was sure he could keep them.

This story first appeared in *Afro SF* and subsequently in *The Apex Book of World SF: Volume 4*.

Chinelo Onwualu is a writer, editor, and journalist living in Abuja, Nigeria. She is a graduate of the 2014 Clarion West Writers Workshop, which she attended as the recipient of the Octavia E. Butler Scholarship. Her writing has appeared in the *Kalahari Review*, *Saraba Magazine*, *Mothership: Tales of Afrofuturism and Beyond*, and elsewhere.

The Apex Book of World SF: Vol 4

Vajra Chandrasekera
Yukimi Ogawa
Zen Cho
Shimon Adaf
Celest Rita Baker
Nene Ormes
JY Yang
Isabel Yap
Usman T. Malik
Kuzhali Manickavel
Elana Gomel
Haralambi Markov
Sabrina Huang
Sathya Stone
Johann Thorsson
Dilman Dila
Swabir Silayi
Deepak Unnikrishnan
Chinelo Onwualu
Saad Z. Hossain
Bernardo Fernández
Nataliam Theodoridou
Samuel Marolla
Julie Novakova
Thomas Old Heuvelt
Sese Yane
Tang Fei
Rocío Rincón

THE APEX BOOK OF WORLD SF

EDITED BY MAHVESH MURAD

4

SERIES EDITOR LAVIE TIDHAR

edited by
Mahvesh Murad

From Spanish steampunk and Italian horror to Nigerian science fiction and subverted Japanese folktales, from love in the time of drones to teenagers at the end of the world, the stories in this volume showcase the best of contemporary speculative fiction, where it's written.

"Important to the future of not only international authors, but the entire SF community."
Strange Horizons

ISBN: 978-1-937009-33-5 ~ ApexBookCompany.com

ROSEWATER
(NOVEL EXCERPT)

TADE THOMPSON

ONE

ROSEWATER: 2066

I'm at the Integrity Bank job for forty minutes before the anxieties kick in. It's how I usually start my day. This time it's because of a wedding and a final exam. Not my wedding, not my exam. In my seat by the window I can see, but not hear, the city. This high above Rosewater everything seems orderly. Blocks, roads, streets, traffic curving sluggishly around the dome. I can see the cathedral from here. The window is to my left, and I'm on one end of an oval table with four other contractors. We are on the fifteenth floor, the top. A skylight is open above us, three-foot square, a security grid being the only thing between us and the morning sky. Blue, with flecks of white cloud. No blazing sun yet, but that will come later. The climate in the room is controlled despite the open skylight, a waste of energy for which Integrity Bank is fined weekly. They are willing to take the expense.

Next to me on the right side Bola yawns. She is pregnant and gets very tired these days. She also eats a lot, but I suppose that's to be expected. I've known her two years and she has been pregnant in each of them. I do not fully understand pregnancy. I am an only child and I never grew up around pets or livestock. My education was peripatetic; biology was never a strong interest. Except for microbiology, which I had to master later.

I try to relax and concentrate on the bank customers. The wedding anxiety comes again.

Rising from the centre of the table is a holographic teleprompter. It consists of random swirls of light right now, but within a few minutes it will come alive with text. There is a room adjacent to ours in which the night shift is winding down.

'I hear they read Dumas last night,' says Bola.

She's just making conversation. It is irrelevant what the other shift reads. I smile and say nothing.

The wedding I sense is due in three months. The bride has put on a few pounds and does not know if she should alter the dress or get liposuction. In my opinion, women have two beauties. The outward appearance that everyone sees and the inner, secret beauty that is true and that women show only to the one they love.

Bola is prettier when she is pregnant.

'Sixty seconds,' says a voice on the tannoy.

I take a sip of water from the tumbler on the table. The other contractors are new. They don't dress formally like Bola and I. They wear tank tops and t-shirts and metal in their hair. They have phone implants.

I hate implants of all kinds. I have one. Standard locator with no add-ons. Boring, really, but my employer demands it.

Publisher's Weekly
Starred Review

Google Play 2016 Book of the Year Editors' Choice

"One of the most imaginative alien invasion scenarios I have come across..."
—Aliette de Bodard, Nebula and BSFA award-winning author of THE HOUSE OF SHATTERED WINGS

"This thrilling, ambitious novel offers a deftly woven and incisive blend of science fiction, psychology, action, and mystery. Highly recommended."
—Kate Elliott, author of BLACK WOLVES and COLD MAGIC

Sometimes sci-fi is thought-provoking because the gaps in its invented world challenge your imagination, but Rosewater is just the opposite: a book so carefully and thoughtfully crafted that you'll be left thinking about it for days.
—Google Play 2016 Editors' Choice

"One of the most imaginative alien invasion scenarios I have come across..."
Aliette de Bodard, Nebula and BSFA award-winning author of *The House of Shattered Wings*

Between meeting a boy who bursts into flames, alien floaters that want to devour him, and a butterfly woman who he has sex with when he enters the xenosphere, Kaaro's life is far from the simple one he wants. But he left simple behind a long time ago when he was caught stealing and nearly killed by an angry mob. Now he works for a government agency called Section 45, and they want him to find a women known as Bicycle Girl. And that's just the beginning.

An alien entity lives beneath the ground, forming a biodome around which the city of Rosewater thrives. The cities of Rosewater are enamored by the dome, hoping for a chance to meet the beings within or possibly be invited to come in themselves. But Kaaro isn't so enamored. He was in the biodome at one point and decided to leave it behind. When something begins killing off other sensitives like himself, Kaaro defies Section 45 to search for an answer, facing his past and comes to a realization about a horrifying future.

ISBN 978-1-937009-29-8   AVAILABLE AS EBOOK AND TRADE PAPERBACK   APEX BOOK COMPANY

The exam anxiety dies down before I can isolate and explore the source. Fine by me.

The bits of metal these young ones have in their hair come from plane crashes. Lagos, Abuja, Jos, Kano, and all points in between, there have been downed aircraft on every domestic route in Nigeria since the early 2000s. They wear bits of fuselage as protective charms.

There are those among us who are shining ones. We know them on sight-we are caught in a vortex and drawn to them as are everyone else. Bola is one of these. I often catch myself staring at her without knowing why. She often catches me staring at her and winks. Now she unwraps her snack, a few wraps of moin-moin.

'Go,' says the tannoy.

The text of Plato's *The Republic* scrolls slowly and steadily in ghostly, holographic figures on the cylindrical display. I start to read, as do the others, some silently, others out loud. We enter the xenosphere and set up the bank's firewall.

Every day about five hundred customers carry out financial transactions at these premises. Wild sensitives probe and push, trying to pick personal data out of the air. I'm talking about dates-of-birth, PINs, mothers' maiden names, past transactions, all of them lying docile in each customer's forebrain, in the working memory, waiting to be plucked out by the hungry, untrained, and freebooting sensitives.

Contractors like myself, Bola Martinez, and the metalheads are trained to repel these. And we do. We read classics to flood the xenosphere with irrelevant words and thoughts, a firewall of knowledge that even makes its way to the subconscious of the customer. A professor did a study of it once. He found a correlation between the material used for firewalling and the activities of the customer for the rest of the year. A person who had never read Shakespeare would suddenly find snatches of *King Lear* coming to mind for no apparent reason.

We can trace the intrusions if we want, but Integrity isn't interested. It's difficult and expensive to prosecute crimes perpetuated in the xenosphere.

The queues for cash machines, so many people, so many cares and wants and passions. I am tired of filtering the lives of others through my mind.

I went down yesterday to the Piraeus with Glaucon the son of Ariston, that I might offer up my prayers to the goddess; and also because I wanted to see in what manner they would celebrate the festival, which was a new thing. I was delighted with the procession of the inhabitants; but that of the Thracians was equally, if not more, beautiful. When we had finished our prayers and viewed the spectacle, we turned in the direction of the city …

On entering the xenosphere there is a projected self-image. The untrained, wild sensitives project themselves, but professionals like me are trained to create a controlled, chosen self-image. Mine is a gryphon.

The wild ones have self-images that are not accurate, that do not map to their current selves. It is not deliberate. It takes time for a mental image to correspond to the actual person, although it varies with individuals. A bald man may have a more hirsute self-image for years.

My first attack of the day comes from a middle-aged man from a town house in Yola. He looks reedy and very dark-skinned. I warn him and he backs off. A teenager takes his place so quickly that I think they are in the same physical location as part of a hack farm. Criminal cabals sometimes round up sensitives, yoke them together in a 'Mumbai-combo'-a call-centre model with serial blackhats.

Either way, I've seen it all before. I am already bored.

During the lunch break one of the metalheads comes in and sits by me. He starts to talk shop, telling me of a near-miss intrusion. He looks to be in his twenties, still excited about being a sensitive, finding everything new and fresh and interesting, the opposite of cynical, the opposite of me.

He must be in love. His self-image shows propinquity. He is good enough to mask the other person, but not good enough to mask the fact of his closeness. I see the shadow, the ghost beside him. I don't mention this out of respect.

The metal he carries is twisted into crucifixes and attached to a single braid on otherwise short hair. This leaves his head on the left temple and coils around his neck, disappearing into the collar of his shirt.

'I'm Clement,' he says. 'I notice you don't use my name.'

This is true. I was introduced to him by an executive two weeks back, but I forgot his name instantly and have been using pronouns ever since.

'My name …'

'You're Kaaro. I know. Everybody knows you. Excuse me for this, but I have to ask. Is it true that you've been inside Utopicity?'

'That's a rumour,' I say.

'Yes, but is the rumour true?' asks Clement.

Outside the window the sun is far too slow in its journey across the sky. Why am I here? What am I doing?

'I'd rather not discuss it.'

'Are you going tonight?' he asks.

I know what night it is. I have no interest in going. 'Perhaps,' I say. 'I might be busy.'

'Doing what?'

This boy is rather nosy. I had hoped for a brief, polite exchange, but now I find myself having to concentrate on him, on my answers. He is smiling, being friendly, sociable. I should reciprocate.

'I'm going with my family,' says Clement. 'Why don't you come with us? I'm sending my number to your phone. All of Rosewater will be there.'

That is the part that bothers me, but I say nothing to Clement. I accept his phone number, and send mine out of politeness, but I do not commit.

Before the end of the working day I get four other invitations to the Opening. I decline most of them, but Bola is not a person I can refuse.

'My husband has rented a flat for the evening,' she says, handing me a slip of paper with the address. Her look of disdain tells me if I had the proper implant we would not need to kill trees. 'Don't eat. I'll cook.'

By eighteen hundred hours the last customer has left and we're all typing at terminals, logging the intrusion attempts, cross-referencing to see if there are any hits, and too tired to joke. We never get feedback on the incident reports. There's no pattern analysis or trend graph. This data is sucked into a bureaucratic black hole. It's just getting dark, and we're all in our own heads now, but passively connected to the xenosphere. I'm vaguely aware that a chess game is going on, but I don't care between whom. I don't play so I don't understand the progress.

'Hello, Gryphon,' someone says.

I focus, but it's gone. She's gone. Definitely female. I get a wispy impression of a flower in bloom, something blue, but that's it. I'm too tired or lazy to follow it up, so I punch in my documentation and fill out the electronic time sheet.

I ride the elevator to street level. I have never seen much of the bank. The contractors have access to the express elevator. It's unmarked and operated by a security guard who sees us, even though we do not see him or his camera. This may as well be magic. The elevator seems like a rather elegant wooden box. There are no buttons and it is unwise to have confidential conversations in there. This time as I leave the operator says, 'Happy Opening.' I nod, unsure of which direction to respond in.

The lobby is empty, dark. Columns stand like Victorian dead posed for pictures. The place is usually manned when I go home, but I expect the staff have been allowed to leave early for the Opening.

It's full night now. The glow from Utopicity's dome is omnipresent, though not bright enough to read by. The skyline around me blocks direct view, but the light frames every high rise to my left like a rising sun, and is reflected off the ones to my right. This is the reason there are no street lights in Rosewater. I make for Alaba Station, the clockwise platform. The streets are empty save the constable who walks past, swinging her baton. I am wearing a suit so she does not care to harass me. A mosquito whines past my ear, but does not appear to be interested in tasting my blood. By the time I reach the concourse there is a patch of light sweat in each of my armpits. It's a warm night. I text my flat to reduce internal temperature one degree lower than external.

Alaba Station is crowded with commercial district workers and the queues snake out to the streets, but they are almost all going anticlockwise to Kehinde Station which is closest to the Opening. I hesitate briefly before I buy my ticket. I plan to go home and change, but I wonder if it will be difficult to meet up with Bola and her husband. I have a brief involuntary connection to the xenosphere and a hot, moist surge of anger from a cuckolded husband lances through me. I disconnect and breathe deeply.

I go home. Even though I have a window seat and the dome is visible, I do not look at Utopicity. When I notice the reflected light on the faces of other passengers I close my eyes, though this does not keep out the savoury smell of akara or the sound of their trivial conversation. There's a saying that everybody in Rosewater dreams of Utopicity at least once every night, however briefly. I know this is not true because I have never dreamed of the place.

That I have somewhere to sit on this train is evidence of the draw of the Opening. The carriages are usually full to bursting and hot, not from heaters, but from body heat and exhalations and despair.

I come off at Atewo after a delay of twenty-five minutes due to a power failure from the north ganglion. I look around for Yaro, but he's nowhere to be found. Yaro's a friendly stray dog who sometimes follows me home and whom I feed scraps. I walk from the station to my block, which takes ten minutes. When I get signal again my phone has four messages. Three of them are jobs. The forth is from my employer.

'Call now. And get a phone implant. This is prehistoric.'

I do not call her. She can wait.

I live in a two-bed, partially automated flat. I could

get a better place if I wanted. I have the funds, but not the inclination. I strip, leaving my clothes where they lie, and pick out something casual. I stare at my gun holster, undecided. I cross the room to the wall safe which appears in response to signals from my ID implant. I open it and consider taking my gun. There are two clips of ammo beside it along with a bronze mask and a clear cylinder. The fluid in the cylinder is at rest. I pick it up and shake it, but the liquid is too viscous and it stays in place. I put it back and decide against a weapon.

I shower briefly and head out to the Opening.

§

How to talk about the Opening?

It is the formation of a pore in the biodome that covers Utopicity. Rosewater is a doughnut-shaped conurbation that surrounds Utopicity. In the early days we actually called it The Doughnut. I was there. I saw it grow from a frontier town of tents and clots of sick people huddling together for warmth into a kind of shanty town of hopefuls and from there into an actual municipality. In its eleven years of existence Utopicity has not taken in a single outsider. I was the last person to traverse the biodome and there will not be another. Rosewater, on the other hand, is the same age, and grows constantly.

Every year, though, the biodome opens for twenty or thirty minutes in the south, in the Kehinde area. All the people in the vicinity of the opening are cured of all physical and some mental ailments. It is also well-known and documented that the outcome is not always good, even if diseases are abolished. There are reconstructions that go wrong, as if the blueprints are warped. Nobody knows why this happens, but there are also people who deliberately injure themselves for the sole purpose of getting "reconstructive surgery."

Trains are out of the question on a night like this. I take a taxi which drives in the opposite direction first, then describes a wide, southbound arc, taking a circuitous route through the back roads and against the flow of traffic. This works until it doesn't. Too many cars and motorbikes and bicycles, too many people walking, too many street performers and preachers and out-of-towners. I pay the driver and walk the rest of the way to Bola's temporary address. This is easy as my path is perpendicular to the crush of pilgrims.

Oshodi Street is far enough from the biodome that the people are not so dense as to impede my progress. Number fifty-one is a tall, narrow four-storey building. The first door is propped open with an empty wooden beer crate. I walk into a hallway that leads to two flats and an elevator. On the top floor, I knock, and Bola lets me in.

One thing hits me immediately: the aroma and heat blast of food which triggers immediate salivation and the drums of hunger in my stomach. Bola hands me field glasses and leads me into the living room. There is a similar pair dangling on a strap around her neck. She wears a shirt with the lower buttons open so that her bare gravid belly pokes out. Her heavy breasts push against the two buttons keeping them in check and I wonder how long the laws of physics will allow this. Two children, male and female, about eight or nine, run around, frenetic, giggling, happy.

'Wait,' says Bola. She makes me wait in the middle of the room and returns with a paper plate filled with akara, dodo, and dundu. She leads me by the free hand to the veranda where there are four deck chairs facing the dome. Her husband, Dele, is in one, the next is empty, the third is occupied by a woman I don't know, and the fourth is for me. Dele Martinez is rotund, jolly, but quiet. I've met him many times before and we get along well. Bola introduces the woman as Aminat, a sister, although the way she emphasises the word, this could mean an old friend who is as close as family, not a biological sibling. She's pleasant enough, smiles with her eyes, has her hair drawn back into a bun of sorts, and is casually dressed in jeans, but is perhaps my age or younger. Bola knows I am single and has made it her mission to find me a mate. I don't like this because … well, when people match-make they introduce people to you whom they think are sufficiently like you. Each person they bring is a commentary on how they see you. If I've never liked anyone Bola has introduced me to does that mean she doesn't know me well enough or that she does know me, but I hate myself?

I sit down and avoid talking by eating. I avoid eye-contact by using the binoculars.

The crowd is contained in Sanni Square, usually a wide-open space framed by exploitative shops and travel agents, behind which Oshodi Street lurks. A firework goes off, premature, a mistake. Most leave the celebrations till afterwards. Oshodi Street is a good spot. It's bright from the dome and we are all covered in that creamy blue electric light. Utopicity's shield is not dazzling, and up close you can see a fluid that ebbs and flows just beneath the surface of the barrier.

The glasses are high-end with infra red sensitivity and a kind of optional implant hack that brings up individual detail about whoever I focus on, tag information travelling by laser dot and information downloading from satellite. It is a bit like being in the xenosphere; I turn it off because it reminds me of work.

Music wafts up, carried in the night, but unpleasant and cacophonic because it comes from competing religious factions, bombastic individuals and the dome tourists. It is mostly percussion-accompanied chanting.

There are, by my estimate, thousands of people. They are of all colours and creeds: black Nigerians, Arabs, Japanese, Pakistani, Persians, white Europeans, and a mix-mash of others. All hope to be healed or changed in some specific way. They sing and pray to facilitate the opening. The dome is, as always, indifferent to their reverence or sacrilege.

Some hold a rapt, religious awe on their faces and cannot bring themselves to talk, while others shout in a continuous, sustained manner. An Imam has suspended himself from a roof in a harness that looks homemade, and is preaching through a bullhorn. His words are lost in the din which swallows meaning and nuance and shits out a homogenous roar. Fights break out but are quashed in seconds because nobody knows if you have to be "good" to deserve the blessings from Utopicity.

A barricade blocks access to the dome and armed constables form up in front of it. The first civilians are one hundred metres away from Utopicity's dome, held back by an invisible stanchion. The officers look like they will shoot to kill. This is something they have done in the past, the latest incident being three years back when the crowd showed unprecedented rowdiness. Seventeen dead, although the victims rose during that year's Opening. They were … destroyed two weeks later as they clearly were not themselves anymore. This happens. Utopicity can restore the body, but not the soul. The god told me that back in '55.

I cough from the peppery heat of the akara. The fit drives my vision to the sky briefly and I see a waning gibbous, battling bravely against the light pollution.

I see the press, filming, correspondents talking into microphones. Here and there are lay-scientists with big scanners pointed finger-like towards Utopicity. Skeptics, true believers, in-between, all represented.

I feel a gentle tap on my left shoulder and emerge from the vision. Aminat is looking at me. Bola and her husband have shifted out of earshot.

'What do you see?' she asks. She is smiling as if she is in on some joke but unsure if it's at my expense.

'People desperate for healing,' I say. 'What do you see?'

'Poverty,' says Aminat. 'Spiritual poverty.'

'What do you mean?'

'Nothing. Maybe humankind was meant to be sick from time to time. Maybe there is something to be learned from illness.'

'Are you politically inclined against Utopicity?'

'No, hardly. I don't have politics. I just like to examine all angles of an issue. Do you care?'

I shake my head. I don't want to be here, and if not for Bola's invitation I would be home contemplating my cholesterol levels. I am intrigued by Aminat, but not enough to want to access her thoughts. She is trying to make conversation, but I don't like talking about Utopicity. Why then do I live in Rosewater? I should move to Lagos, Abuja, Accra, anywhere but here.

'I don't want to be here either,' says Aminat.

I wonder for a moment if she has read my thoughts, if Bola matched us because she is also a sensitive. That would be irritating.

'Let's just go through the motions to keep Bola happy. We can exchange numbers at the end of the evening and never call each other again. I will tell her tomorrow, when she asks, that you were interesting and attentive, but there was no chemistry. And you will say …?'

'That I enjoyed my evening, and I like you, but we didn't quite click.'

'You will also say that I had wonderful shoes and magnificent breasts.'

'Er … okay.'

'Good. We have a deal. Shake on it?'

Except, we cannot shake hands because there is oil on mine from the akara, but we touch the back of our hands together, co-conspirators. I find myself smiling at her.

A horn blows and we see a dim spot on the dome, the first sign. The dark spot grows into a patch. I have not seen this as often as I should. I saw it the first few times but stopped bothering after five years.

The patch is roughly circular, with a diameter of six or seven feet. Black as night, as charcoal, as pitch. It looks like those dark bits on the surface of the sun. This is the boring part. It will take half an hour for the first healing to manifest. Right now all is invisible. Microbes flying into the air. The scientists are frenzied now. They take air samples and will try to grow cultures on blood agar. Futile. The xenoforms do not grow on artificial media.

In the balcony everyone except me takes a deep breath, trying to get as much inside their lungs as possible. Aminat breaks her gaze from the dome, twists in her seat and kisses me on the lips. It lasts seconds and nobody else sees it, intent as they are upon the patch. After a while I am not sure it happened at all. I don't even know what to make of it. I can read minds but I still don't understand women.

Down below it begins, the first cries of rapture. It is

impossible to confirm or know what ailments are taken care of at first. If there is no obvious deformity or stigmata like jaundice, pallor, or a broken bone, there is no visible change except the emotional state of the healed. Already, down at front, younger pilgrims are doing cartwheels and crying with gratitude.

A man brought in on a stretcher gets up. He is wobbly at first, but then walks confidently. Even from this distance I can see the wideness and wildness of his eyes and the rapid flapping of his lips. Newcomers experience disbelief.

This continues in spurts and sometimes ripples that flow through the gathered people. The trivial and the titanic are equally healed.

The patch is shrinking now. At first the scientists and I are the only ones to notice. Their activities become more agitated. One of them shouts at the others, though I cannot tell why.

I hear a tinkle of laughter from beside me. Aminat is laughing with delight, her hands held half an inch from her face and both cheeks moist. She is sniffing. That's when it occurs to me that she is here to be healed as well.

I get a text at that moment. I look at my palm to read the message off the flexible subcutaneous polymer. My boss again.

Call right now, Kaaro. I am not kidding.

TWO

ROSEWATER: 2066

It's the middle of the night when I arrive at Ubar. I come off the last train and there's a car waiting for me. Ubar is an area between the North Ganglion and the widest part of the River Yemoja. We drive along the banks before turning away into empty roads and dark buildings. The driver stops in front of imposing iron gates and waits for me to get out, then drives off.

I walk into a facility that belongs to the Ministry of Agriculture. From the outside it is a simple, two-storey building with ordinary signage showing the Nigeria Coat-of-Arms covered in dust. Inside there's a reception and an open plan office. There are framed photographs of the president on one wall and Rosewater's mayor Jack Jacques on the other. Mundane. I'm

buzzed through all of this without delay and my RFID is logged sure as cancer.

I go straight to the elevator down to the sub-levels. These are used and controlled by Section Forty-five, or S45. Most have never heard of this obscure branch of government. I have only heard of them because I work for them. Before that I was a finder and a thief.

Part of my job with S45 is interrogation. I hate interrogations.

It is 0300 hours and we are in a dim meeting room. There are two agents in black suits standing on either side of a prisoner who is naked and tied to a chair. The prisoner is blindfolded. The agents don't speak and I do not know what information they need. I don't bother trying to read them because the organisation would not have sent them if they knew anything. This is part of some bureaucrat's idea of keeping the subject's mind uncontaminated with expectations. What they want is for me to copy all the information from the subject's mind, like making a backup of a hard drive. This is ridiculous and not possible, but no matter how many times I've written memos to the powers that be, this continues to be the manner in which they request interrogation.

Data does not spool into or out of the brain like a recording.

The man in front of me is black, unbruised, breathing in ragged hitches, and muscular. From time to time he says 'please' in Kanuri or Hausa. He tries Igbo and Yoruba sometimes, but I am not convinced he speaks any of the languages fluently. I am uncomfortable and stay two feet away from him. I connect to the xenosphere. I first establish that he is not a sensitive. His self-image is the same as the man in the chair. That's good — it means I will not be here all night.

There is violence in this man's head. I see two men beating a third in what looks like a backyard. The two men alternate kicks and punches between them while their victim tries to stay upright, using his forearms to shield himself as best as can be managed. The victim is bruised, dirty, and bleeding from the mouth and nose. He does not seem afraid. If anything, he appears to be mocking his tormentors. His attackers are uniformed, dark-skinned, with berets and sunglasses designed to make them seem identical. They do not look like the Nigerian police or Army, at least not by the uniform. Looking closer, the uniforms seem homemade, like from one of the militia. They have no weapons holsters, but one has a pistol stuck in a belt at the small of his back.

Something else that is odd: I cannot smell the yard or taste the dust that the three men kick up. I have neither the taste of blood in my mouth as the victim should, nor the pain of impact on my knuckles as the perpetuators should. Instead, this image is associated with the taste of food and drink, specifically kuli-kuli and beer. I also keep getting snatches of music from a cheap keyboard.

I briefly emerge from the xenosphere and inspect the prisoner. I walk around behind him and check his bound hands. His knuckles are dark, callused. You get this from knuckle push-ups and punching a hard surface like a wall or Wooden Man in order to remove sensation from the area, to make you a better fighter. I know this because I have done it. I check this because none of the participants in the prisoner's memory seemed trained in hand-to-hand. He is not one of them.

Did he order the beating? Where did he witness it from?

Then it hits me.

'Oh, you clever bastard,' I say.

I re-enter the xenosphere. The 'memory' is staged. The prisoner watched it in a movie on repeat and was probably eating and drinking at the same time. He probably found a lesser known Nollywood film, which accounts for the cheesy music and the poor production values. He is not a sensitive, but he knows we exist and that he might be exposed to one on arrest. What it means to me is that he does have something to hide. I probe at the edges of the memory, which is like trying to peel off the adhesive label on a packet. I need to find purchase. I fix not on the image or sound, but on the other senses. Touch, smell, taste.

'Hello, Gryphon.'

It's the same woman as earlier in the night while I was at the bank, playful, curious, ephemeral. The interruption breaks my concentration and I see the beating looping around and around. I search for a linked self-image but all I can find is the noise of the general xenosphere. Random mentations. Useless. I am irritated, but my training kicks in and I focus my will on the matter at hand.

The sensation associated with the beating is gentle pressure on the buttocks and food, which tells me he was seated in some living room watching the scene on a wide-screen TV or a hologram. I discover the smell of cigarette smoke. The scene shifts, wobbles, dissipates and I'm in a smoke-filled room with five other men, all of whom are intent on the screen. Nobody speaks, but they drink beer, they smoke, and they chew the snacks laid out on a tray.

I don't like interrogations, but I'm good at them. I feel proud of myself when I solve a puzzle, and then I feel disgust. I try to think of myself as a lawyer, operating within certain parameters that do not include morality. Focus on the task.

I pull out and say to the agents, 'I need a forensic sketch artist. Now.'

I am debriefed by my boss, Femi Alaagomeji. Video-conference, of course. Nobody in the security services would ever knowingly be in the same room with a sensitive. I know for a fact that they are not even allowed to form relationships with sensitives and are required to report the occurrence of sensitives in their families. The last time I breathed the same air as Femi was six years ago, but before that was eleven years ago, when she shoved me into S45, just before my training, when Utopicity was new and Rosewater was nascent.

Femi is the most beautiful woman I have ever seen. She is physically perfect in so many ways it hurts. In a sterile room, with a secure link, I videoconference with her. Today she wears burgundy lipstick. I happen to know she has a burgundy convertible Mercedes Benz. She must have driven it to work today.

'Kaaro,' she says.

'Femi,' I say.

'Call me Mrs Alaagomeji.'

'Femi.'

This is an old dance that we dance. She is not really irritated and I am not really impudent. We play the roles all the same.

'Who is the prisoner, Femi?'

'Classified, need-to-know, all that good shit. What do you have for me?'

'Faces. Five of them. The artist did well and is running them through the system right now. She's also looking at the location, the brand of the electronics, everything. That's all for today. I'm tired and it's almost time for my day job.'

'It's not a job. You contract. This is your job.'

'Fine. My other job.'

'How long will it take?'

'I do not know. If you told me his name —'

'No.'

'— or what he's done —'

'No.'

'Then we do it the hard way, inch by inch. I discover information, I stop, I let the artist know, we start again.'

'So be it.'

'Can I go home now?'

'In a minute. How are you, Kaaro?'

'I'm fine.'

'You're lonely.'

'I am alone, not lonely. It's solitude, but that doesn't have to be a bad thing. I'm keeping up with my reading. I'm going to learn to play the oboe.'

'What are you reading?'

'Chomsky.'

'All right. Are you really learning the oboe?'

'No.'

'I don't know why I bother asking. Go home.'

'Goodnight, Femi.'

§

I'm barely able to keep my eyes open by the time the S45 car drops me at home. The night has lost the battle with the day and soon Rosewater will rise and go to work. The city wakes up in layers. Food comes first. Long haul drivers bring in crops from Oyo, Ogbomosho, Ilorin, and Abeokuta. Cassava, corn, yam flour, millet, rice from Thailand. Not a lot sourced locally anymore. These are delivered to the many categories of Bukka, the Mama Put, the Food-is-ready. Cheap, local, and essential for the unskilled workers who need a hearty carbohydrate bomb before tackling their less-than-minimum wage jobs where they go to use their biceps, triceps, and spinal columns to lift, hew, saw, join, shave, slaughter, and clean. They cook. The aroma draws out the first tier of office worker, clerks, secretaries, juniors. Over a two-hour period the middle-class professionals of Rosewater will arrive at their offices, surgeries, law chambers, accounting firms, and of course banks.

I will be joining them, but I need a shower and breakfast, perhaps strong coffee. I live in the middle floor of a three-storey in Atewo. An eight-digit code opens my flat, but there is an override key.

A series of phone messages come through as if the signal just became strong enough. I seriously consider skipping the bank, pretending to be sick and sleeping all day. I want to find out who is trying to reach me across the xenosphere. I strip and walk naked into the shower. I try that trick of using warm, then cold, then scalding hot water, but it does not refresh me. In the mirror my eyes look bloodshot and baggy like they're from a pervert's mug shot.

'You look like an idiot,' I say to my reflection. 'You *are* an idiot. Your life is meaningless.'

I put on boxers and pad into the living room without getting fully dry.

'Miles Davis, "So What,"' I say to the sensors and the base plucks out on the speakers.

'Phone, messages.'

I sit. I close my eyes. I listen.

My accountant wants to discuss my taxes.

The National Research Laboratory calls. They want three days of my time. They will pay. I will ignore them. I have worked for them before and I don't want to anymore. They're in Lagos and they want to know about sensitives. I hate going to Lagos and the NRL scientists stare at me as if they want to open my brain while I'm still alive.

A message from Aminat, her speech like musical chairs. 'Hello, Kaaro. I know, I know, we were only going through the motions. But I find myself thinking of you and I wonder what … (laughter) Oh, God, this is so … Okay, call back. Or not. I'm not as needy as I sound.'

She has me smiling.

A television producer who has been hounding me for two years offers me money and fame if I will appear on *Nigeria is Talented*.

'Hello, Gryphon.'

I first think the person has left me a message on my phone but that's not it. I open my eyes and a shoal of mackerel, oku eko, fly past my face. Miles still plays the horn, but it sounds distant. I am in a place of shifting colours and shadows. I look down at my hands and they are gone. Instead, there are feathers.

This shit hasn't happened to me in a long time. I am in the xenosphere-asleep and in the xenosphere. It's easy to see how. Warm bath, sleep deprivation.

'Gryphon.'

'Who are you?' I ask, against all of my training.

'I like your plumage,' she says. 'Can you fly?'

'Anybody can fly here. Who are you?'

The fish are beginning to bother me. The air has the consistency of water. I hear an underhum of voices and thoughts of others at low signal. I cannot see this woman although I hear her clearly. No self image?

'I am an individual,' she says. 'I am a one.'

'Yes, but what's your name? Ki l'oruko e?'

'Must I have one?'

'Yes.'

She is silent for a time. I try to scratch my face, but I tickle myself with feathers instead. I stretch my wings and it feels better.

'My name is Molara,' she says.

I snap up one of the mackerels in my beak and break its back, then drop it to the floor between my forepaws. It twitches and lies still.

'Show yourself,' I say.

'I don't know how,' said Molara.

Definitely a wild strain. I speak, echoing the words of my instructor.

'Think of something you love, something you hate, something you fear, something disgusting or beautiful. Something you find impressive.'

Fire trucks of all sizes and descriptions stream past, none of their lights flashing. Some of them are toys. Behind each one a red masquerade runs, tiny Lilliputians for the toys, giants for the full-sized.

A butterfly flowers in front of my face. It unfolds lengthwise with a fourteen-foot wingspan. It is black and blue and its wings move in a majestic slow beat.

Then I wake, jarred out of the xenosphere at the same time by the phone. I am confused for a moment. The phone stops, then starts again.

'Yes?' I say.

'You're meant to be here,' says Bola. 'You sound hung-over. Are you hung-over?'

'Oh, shit.'

I am monstrously late.

My grooming is sloppy, but better than the metalheads' so I'm fine. The customers surround the bank like ants feeding on a child's dropped lollypop. The day after the Opening is always extra busy because people want to see their doctors and get laboratory tests to confirm their healing. The Rosewater medical community is not very robust and comes alive only at this time of year. One would think they would be out of practice.

The firewall is up without me. They are reading pages of Tolstoy. I sit in the break room and rub ketoconazole cream on my exposed skin to keep me out of the xenosphere. It's the busiest banking day of the year and I do not want to fatigue myself further. I drink horrendous instant coffee by the cupful to keep myself awake, a benched striker.

INTERLUDE: MISSION

LAGOS: 2060

It is unbearably hot, but still I wait. I feel rivulets of sweat dripping down my back, in between my butt cheeks. I can just about breathe, but the close, oxygen poor air threatens to make me black out. There are moth balls here waxing aromatic in my nose and mind, whispering fact and fiction about my wife. I can barely keep still. The clothes in the closet caress my back. Down around my feet there are shoes crowding, jostling for space. A dangling belt tinkles with my movements, made loud by the silence. My left hand rests against the warm wood of the door, my right by my side, weighed down by the knife.

I wait.

Any moment now.

I hear a door slam from elsewhere in the house. I hear the beep as the door autolocks, and giggling that makes me see red. Literally, red flashes across my eyes in the darkness, like a surge of blood, just for a second. I can feel my heart driving the blood through my body, demanding that I move. I wait.

There are bumps and mistakes as two people wind their way through my house, through our house. The door to the room swings open. I imagine them standing there kissing. I hear the sucking sound of their lips. My fist tightens on the handle of the blade.

'Stop,' says my wife, but she is laughing.

'Okay. No means no,' says the man, mock seriousness.

Her perfume reaches me now. I hear the adulterous rustle of her clothes falling to the carpet.

'Really?' says my wife.

Now the blood sings in my ears. My head feels larger and my mouth is completely dry. I feel my scrotum constrict.

Lydia, Lydia, Lydia.

I do not know if I am thinking this or if her lover is repeating her name over, but her first gasp of pleasure is my cue.

I break out of the closet. The first few seconds are free because they do not hear me in their passion. I am at the bed. She is naked, supine, legs apart. He is between those legs, his hand buried in her sex, his neck beginning to turn.

I cut him first, side of the neck, surgical. The blood spurts, but I ignore it and shove him by the right arm. Lydia screams. Her eyes are rather comical circles, the whites larger than I have ever seen. For spite I drive the knife into her left eye, withdraw it, then stab her throat. I look at the man who is holding his neck and wetting the carpet with his blood. His shirt is soaked. His movements lack direction and he will die soon. I turn back to Lydia who is gurgling now.

I take my time to —

I vomit.

I fall to all fours and spew yellow-green slime. 'Oh, fuck. He did it,' I say.

Ohfuckohfuckohfuck.

'Are you sure?' asks Femi. 'No hair, no DNA, no physical evidence.'

I cough. 'Holy fucking shit, Femi, if I say he did it, he did it. He did it, okay? I fucking did it.'

'Kaaro, calm down.' She places a hand on my back,

but I shrug it off.

'I did it. I bought a Gene-grub and let it feed on me, then I let it loose in the room after I killed them both. An elegant drone hack removed traces of me from surveillance cameras. I paid the staff of the hotel for their blindness. I drowned them in a river of foreign currency. They will go to their deathbeds denying that they ever set eyes on me.'

I dry heave.

'Kaaro, you mean him, right?'

Oh fuck, the revulsion. Oh, fuck. Ori mi. Help! Lydia! Lydia!

Why the fuck does it feel like … Why am I guilty?

'Help me,' I say. 'Help me.'

I crawl into a corner. I cannot stop shaking; I cannot stop seeing my arm rise and fall, the wide eyes, the gurgling …

'Over-identification,' says the doctor. I forget his name, I do not like him.

Three months since the assignment. I am sequestered, back in from the cold, as they say. They stick me in a mental joint, for field agents who go over the edge, and I most definitely went over the edge.

He continues. 'You identified too strongly with your subject. Ego boundaries blurred and you lost the integrity of your self. You thought you were him.'

'I know that here,' I say, pointing to my head, 'but not in my heart.'

He laughs. 'That's an improvement over when you first arrived. If it's in your head, your heart will follow.'

I am not so sure. I am not so sure who I am. I mean, I know I am Kaaro, and I work for S45 and I was trained by Professor Ileri and Rosewater is my home and … but … but I *remember* how Lydia sighs after fucking just before she demands that I get her a glass of water. I remember sliding the ring on her finger the day we get married. The biodome is a mixture of cerulean and vanilla in the background of our wedding photos. I remember her cooking. I remember opening a sauce pan to see the stew bubbling, gurgling, like the froth from her neck when I …

I feel the tear roll down my cheek. 'Doc, I miss her,' I say. 'If I never met her, why do I miss her so much? Why do I feel guilty?'

'Maybe you feel guilty because there is someone you, Kaaro, have an unconscious desire to kill. The murder of Lydia fulfilled that desire. Down under the surface of our mind lie the demons and gremlins of our base instincts, struggling for expression.' He checks the screen in front of him and asks, 'Have you been taking the meds?'

No. 'Yes.' No. They make me impotent.

'This is the third antidepressant we've tried. I've never seen such a strong reaction. Ileri thinks it's because your ability is more acute than any other.'

'My wife is dead. I should be sad, right?' I ask.

'Kaaro, you have never been married. You never even met Lydia. You spent time in her homicidal husband's mind. The experience was so intense that you can't disconnect. The pills aren't working. I'd like to try something else.'

He slides over consent forms for shock treatment.

I walk out of the building.

I really want a cigarette, even though I have not smoked for a long time. I just feel like I should be smoking.

Nine months. I have lost enough time to have a baby.

A drone descends to read my identity, then flies off.

I get a phone call. It's Femi, so I ignore it. Great service to your country blah blah put the man in jail for life blah blah sacrifice, sacrifice, sacrifice, blah blah.

I cannot remember everything that happened, gaps in my memory. A part of me thinks perhaps there is a reason for the gaps and that I really do not want to know.

There's a sorrow in me, though. I do not know why, but I feel it.

Whatever they pay me is not enough.

I look for a taxi.

(excerpt ends)

Rosewater *by Tade Thompson is available now from Apex Book Company and your favorite book vendors.*

Art used on p. 80 copyright 2016 Tade Thompson

Tade Thompson lives and works in the UK. He is the author of a number of SFF, crime, general fiction, and memoir pieces. His alternate history crime novel *Making Wolf* from Rosarium Publishing was released in September, 2015.

SEEKING TANIS. RUNNER AVAILABLE

BETSY PHILLIPS

I can't remember where I first heard about *The Black Tapes*, the creepy *X-Files* meets *Serial* podcast produced by Pacific Northwest Stories, but I can distinctly remember finishing the first episode and then having to immediately replay it because I could not believe what I had just heard. Not in the sense of "Is this real or not?"—though that was a question I initially had—but in the sense of "Who are these people? How did they pull this off?"

In a world full of podcasts that strives to be frightening, *The Black Tapes* stands out for actually achieving those scares.

The host of the podcast is Alex Reagan, who, along with her producer, Nic Silver, is investigating supernatural incidents centered around the mysterious black video tapes collected by the enigmatic skeptic, Dr. Richard Strand. The stories range from unsettling—a father and son

are both followed by a large indistinct smudge—to the spookily fascinating—a high-school bullying incident transforms into a legend of a woman with an upside-down face—to the downright terrifying—The Unsound (For those of you who know what I'm talking about, no more is necessary. For those of you who don't, I won't spoil it.).

At the end of the first season, listeners were introduced to another Pacific Northwest Stories podcast, *Tanis*. *Tanis* is Nic Silver's baby, his exploration of a strange place that may or may not exist, a cross between Jeff VanderMeer's Southern Reach trilogy and that old Christian Slater movie, *Pump Up the Volume*, with the best hacker in pop culture this side of Mr. Robot in MeerKatnip.

Tanis is, perhaps, harder to explain than *The Black Tapes*, but I like it better. Don't get me wrong. I love *The Black Tapes*, but *Tanis* feels more like a story told for people raised in a time when things still could be kept secret. If you have H.P. Lovecraft, Jack Parsons, old cassettes, Christian Slater, long, perhaps pot-fueled, philosophical discussions, and ambivalence about large corporations in your personal constellation of meaningful things, Tanis is going to blow your mind.

Though the two podcasts share the same crew, you can listen to one without having to listen to the other. I think it's worth it to listen to both, since they seem to be trying to get at the same thing—not a literal thing, but a narrative concern—from two different directions. *The Black Tapes* is about Alex's wish that she could find among the ordinary things of life—the birthday parties, the rock bands we like, the coffee shops, the places we might hike—proof of something supernatural and legendary, definitive proof. *Tanis* is about Nic's attempt to take a legend, a supernatural phenomenon, and find ordinary, mundane traces of it in real life.

Both shows are asking us to consider how we might locate the uncanny and how a direct experience of it might change us. The tension between their very different approaches is a necessary part of that consideration, I think.

Executive producers Paul Bae and Terry Miles were kind enough to answer some of my questions and some questions from other Apex readers who are fans of the podcasts.

APEX MAGAZINE: Both *The Black Tapes* and *Tanis* can be quite frightening. For me, as a listener, I've always comforted myself with the knowledge that whatever's happening in a particular episode, obviously, Alex and Nic must be okay because the episode exists (later *Tanis* developments aside). With that in mind, I'm wondering if we can talk about what was, for me, hands down the most terrifying moment of *The Black Tapes*. In Episode 4 of Season 2, the first time I listened to it, Alex messes up one of the Squarespace ads. That screw-up unsettled me so much I had to stop listening and get up and do something else for a minute. It seemed that Alex was so unwell that her problems were leaking over into the framework of the show. It was so unexpected and so scary. The ad's not messed up anymore, though. Why did you choose to fix it?

PNWS: We didn't even notice it before it was uploaded. We get into a work groove here at PNWS studios and when we hear an ad, we kind of skip forward knowing what it's going to be. It wasn't until it was public that one of our staff members asked us about it. That's when we started thinking Alex might seriously need some time off. We fixed it as soon as we could for that reason. It wasn't intentional.

AM: When we're first introduced to Dr. Strand on *The Black Tapes*, it's pretty clear he's universally loathed by the people who know him and he, in return, is less than excited about the rest of humanity. He has now become something of a sex symbol in certain corners of *The Black Tapes* fandom. It must feel to him like the world's opinion of him has flip-flopped. Is that strange for him? Is he even aware of this phenomenon? Does Dr. Strand now have groupies? Would he notice if he did?

PNWS: As far as we know, he has no idea any of that's going on. He's a very focused individual and rarely takes time away from his work. In fact, now that you mention it, we don't remember ever having social time with him. No dinners, drinks, potluck…nothing. We think he'd be confused by the whole thing if we told him.

AM: On *Tanis*, Nic mentions being heavily influenced by Hard Harry from *Pump Up the Volume* and his DIY ethos comes through on the show. Is this podcast enough for him, though? For any of you guys? *Welcome* to *Nightvale* has the traveling show and the books. Limetown recently announced that it's not returning until the creators see if they can make a go of a TV show and they'll also have a book. Aaron Mahnke from *Lore* has a television deal. Any chance that *The Black Tapes* or *Tanis* might outgrow their podcast roots, too?

PNWS: Podcasting is our first love. We made a covenant with our fans who have committed to us and our stories. By creating and releasing these shows, we are asking them to trust us and come along for the ride. We will never break that trust. So, we are hard at work on *The Black Tapes*, *Tanis*, and some new shows that we plan on launching soon. We can say that, we are involved in other mediums, and have been working on all of them from very early on, so stay tuned!

AM: On the Pacific Northwest Stories website, you say, "As most of you have probably already discovered, our former host removed all of our past work from the internet." On Episode 1 of Season 2 of *Tanis*, Nic makes a vague reference to threats being part of the reason he had MeerKatnip remove most traces of him from the internet. For those of us not from the Pacific Northwest and thus who didn't hear the terrestrial radio version of PNWS, could you fill us in on what happened with your former host? This former host isn't the source of some of the threats against Nic, is she or he?

PNWS: By "host" we mean our former bosses, and no, they are definitely not threatening Nic. They are actually notoriously hard to track down and a lot of them are out of the industry, and the former content is owned or co-owned and controlled by a web of corporations and entities. We're trying to gather up as much content and permission(s) as we can, but that process is mired in red

tape. We are hoping to get some of that material. We think some of those older shows could make for great podcast series.

AM: Apex has selected two questions from our readers:

Darcy Little Badger (@shiningcomic) asks the following — *The Black Tapes* and *Tanis* have amassed a fun online community of fans. Personally, I enjoy reading episode discussions on the PNWS subreddit. Has listener feedback/community participation affected the direction PNWS podcasts in any significant way?

PNWS: Our executive producers avoid going to Reddit unless doing an AMA only because they're too busy trying to grow PNWS. As far as we know, no one here does anything more than dip their toes into the discussions there. But we can't be sure about everyone. We love that the community is vibrant, smart and incredibly passionate.

AM: Varo Stiglitz (@alvaromateu) asks the following — Will we see more of Charlie Strand soon? Seems like she just vanished from the series.

PNWS: We can't say…

Don't hesitate. Go listen to *TANIS* and *The Black Tapes* now!

TANIS: www.tanispodcast.com
The Black Tapes: theblacktapespodcast.com

Betsy Phillips is a writer who lives in Whites Creek, Tennessee. Her fiction has appeared in Apex, Fantasy & Science Fiction, and other places. Whenever anything strange happens, her first thought is "Oh, a ghost!" It is almost never a ghost.

COVER ARTIST FOCUS: INTERVIEW WITH SUNNY RAY

RUSSELL DICKERSON

Our cover artist is Sunny Ray, a multifaceted artist working in digital painting and illustration. Many of her pieces are driven by the stories that she loves to write, leading to new paintings and animations. "The Fire," our cover art, is part of a concept for a story about a boy who can use the sky like a touchscreen.

APEX MAGAZINE: On the DeviantArt page for "The Fire," the first comment makes a great point about people staring at their devices these days, adding "we should be looking up, not down." With films like Interstellar offering similar advice, do you hope that someone seeing this piece will be inspired to try something bold? How do you see your work helping others to take a bigger step into new things?

SUNNY RAY: I would like to think it would inspire people to try something bold! I think people may interpret it differently than I do, however, as the basis of the message in my mind as I was painting it is if you are going to go out, you might as well do it with a bang, like a brilliant sunset before the dark. We're only here for a short time, so we might as well go out bright and loud. Either way people interpret this painting, whether it to be looking up and reaching for the stars, or if they interpret it as going out with a bang, I can see this work pushing people to ignore the limits and go the distance!

AM: With being a student of both design and animation, does creating a piece like "Breathing Galaxies" start with the focus on the climactic image, or planning the overall animation and message? How might the message of a piece change over the time the animation takes to run its course, and how does the art style versus the design technique influence that?

SR: To be honest, that piece only really started because I saw a picture of the subject (danisnotonfire) that I really wanted to recreate in an aesthetic style. This was a test of my abilities to not only recreate realism from a photograph but to also add an expectant element of animation in a still imagery. But, usually if I am going to start an animation like that, I have an idea for the image I want to create, then I will play around and try different things with the animation. The message might change depending on the animation or the animation furthers the message. This piece you only see the message because of the animation.

AM: In the descriptions of a few of your DeviantArt pieces, you mention having a rough week. That's something many artists and creators, even in my own personal experience, work through seemingly more than the general public. Does creating new art help you work through any life issues? Are the colors you choose or the style you are creating with affected by your emotions as you work?

SR: Yes, definitely, making art has helped me through my struggle against life. Of course the only reason I have the experience and the passion for art was because of my weakest moments. It's one of my biggest comforts that if everything were to go south, I'd know I'd at least have my art and stories there in the end. For me, however, I don't think my style or the colors I choose are really affected by my emotions as much as the concept of the piece. I have color schemes that I'm partial to, like, I prefer a warmer palette over cool colors.

AM: As a student, you have to often follow particular assignments and plans. When you work on personal pieces that don't have that structure, do you approach the ideas any differently? Do you prefer the openness of your own choices, the rigidness of a structured assignment, or a bit of both?

SR: I jump right into personal projects. It could be three in the morning and if an idea hits me that I like then I will start then and there and work through the night on it. Unfortunately, I do not have quite the same vigor when it comes to my assignments usually because I don't have the openness of the choice. In one of my classes, we were assigned to create a twenty-page magazine featuring articles, ads, and visuals in a group. However, my whole group neglected to show up for class so my teacher let me do the magazine on my own per request. While all the other groups struggled with the rigidity of having to agree on a topic and self-create all the content within the time frame, I flew through that assignment faster than any other assignment because while there were requirements I had to fulfill, I got to make all the choices while the other groups had to adhere to their group decisions.

AM: On the DeviantArt page for your beautiful piece "Fallen Angel," you mention your improvement in painting wings. When you look at your own works, do you look at them more from the aspect of the vision and content, or the techniques that you used to create them? Are there interpretations or critiques of your pieces from others that you wouldn't have expected?

SR: When I look at my work, I think I see both. Sometimes I look back on them to see where the vision and contents came from while other times I will look back to see my technique and how I can improve in future works. I think to use old works as references for future pieces. My friends and followers have told me that my art inspires them, which is something I never had expected my art to be able to do. Other than that, however, I haven't gotten any interpretations or critiques that I wouldn't have expected, or none that come to mind.

About the Artist:
Sunny Ray is studying web design and animation, and plans to continue painting and personal art projects. She also has several stories and books planned for the future, including more about the boy from this month's cover. To see more of her work, visit intothefrisson.deviantart.com and facebook.com/IntotheFrisson.

Russell Dickerson has been a published illustrator and designer since the previous millennium, creating works for many genre publications and authors. He has also written many articles for various organizations in that time, including *Apex*, and his work can be found on his website at www.darkstormcreative.com.

SUNNY RAY GALLERY

To see more visit:
intothefrisson.deviantart.com
facebook.com/IntotheFrisson

Wiley

Fallen Angel

Monica Dream

Eye-based Paternity Testing
& Other Human Genetic Mythis

Dan Koboldt

In 2001, scientists announced an incredible accomplishment: they had completed the sequence of the human genome. The complete instruction book for making a human being spans 24 chromosomes and is 3.2 billion letters long. That's about 1,000 times the length of the first ten Wheel of Time books put together. Sequencing the whole thing had taken ten years and something like eight billion dollars.

That's a considerable investment for the taxpayers, but the scientists made incredible promises. They said it would be the scientific breakthrough of the century. With the sequence of the genome in hand, they promised to dramatically improve the prevention, diagnosis, and treatment of disease. They told us the completion of the human genome would mark a new era for human health.

They lied.

Well, that's not entirely fair. Finishing the genome was the starting point in a long journey to understanding how our genes make us who we are. The more they study it, the more scientists have found that the genome is incredibly complex. I know, because I'm one of them. I work as a human geneticist at one of three large-scale DNA sequencing centers in the United States.

Unfortunately, few things about genetics and inheritance are straightforward. They're certainly not as simple as we often see them portrayed in books, movies, and other media. As a scientist who also enjoys science fiction, I often encounter popular misconceptions about how genetics actually works. Here are a few of the more common (and inaccurate) tropes:

THE EYE-BASED PATERNITY TEST

Oh, if I had a dime for every time a character recognized a long-lost parent or sibling based on eye color, a widow's peak, a peanut allergy, or some other physical quirk. Sure, first-degree relatives do tend to look alike, and many visible traits tend to run in families. Yet they should not be used to establish (or disprove) kinship because it's not that simple.

Eye color, despite the common wisdom suggesting otherwise, is a complex inherited trait. While it's true that blue eyes tend to be recessive and brown eyes tend to be dominant, eye color is a spectrum, not a multiple-choice test. The color of the iris is determined by the amount of melanin in it, and that can be influenced by as many as 10 different genes. Brown-eyed parents can have blue-eyed children and vice-versa. Also, eye color can change: many newborns have blue eyes that become brown or green during early childhood.

Please, don't rely on physical characteristics to tell who's related to whom. The inheritance of such traits does not always follow a predictable pattern. Even when it does, in real life, these kinds of tests might uncover secrets that were better left buried.

When we do genetics studies of families, we verify the expected relationships as a quality control step. About

4% of the time, there's a discrepancy (most often, the reported father is not the biological father). This observation holds true across racial groups and socioeconomic strata, and has been consistently reported by many researchers for over a decade.

We call these "non-paternity events" and, generally speaking, we don't report them back to the study participants.

DIFFERENT PEOPLE WITH DIFFERENT GENES

Often I hear people discussing how someone has "the gene" for some trait or ability. Alternatively, an elderly person in good health is often said to have "good genes." In truth, we all have the same set of about 20,000 genes. In very rare cases, large segments of the genome can be deleted (which removes genes), and usually that's a very bad thing. So the concept of people having "different genes" is not accurate. It's the genetic variation within and around genes that accounts for the differences between us.

That said, I recognize that most people use the term genes colloquially. I don't expect people to start saying, "So you're 95 years old? You must have a really good set of genetic variants in your genome."

While we're on the topic, I should tell you that traditionally defined genes—that is, things that code for pro-

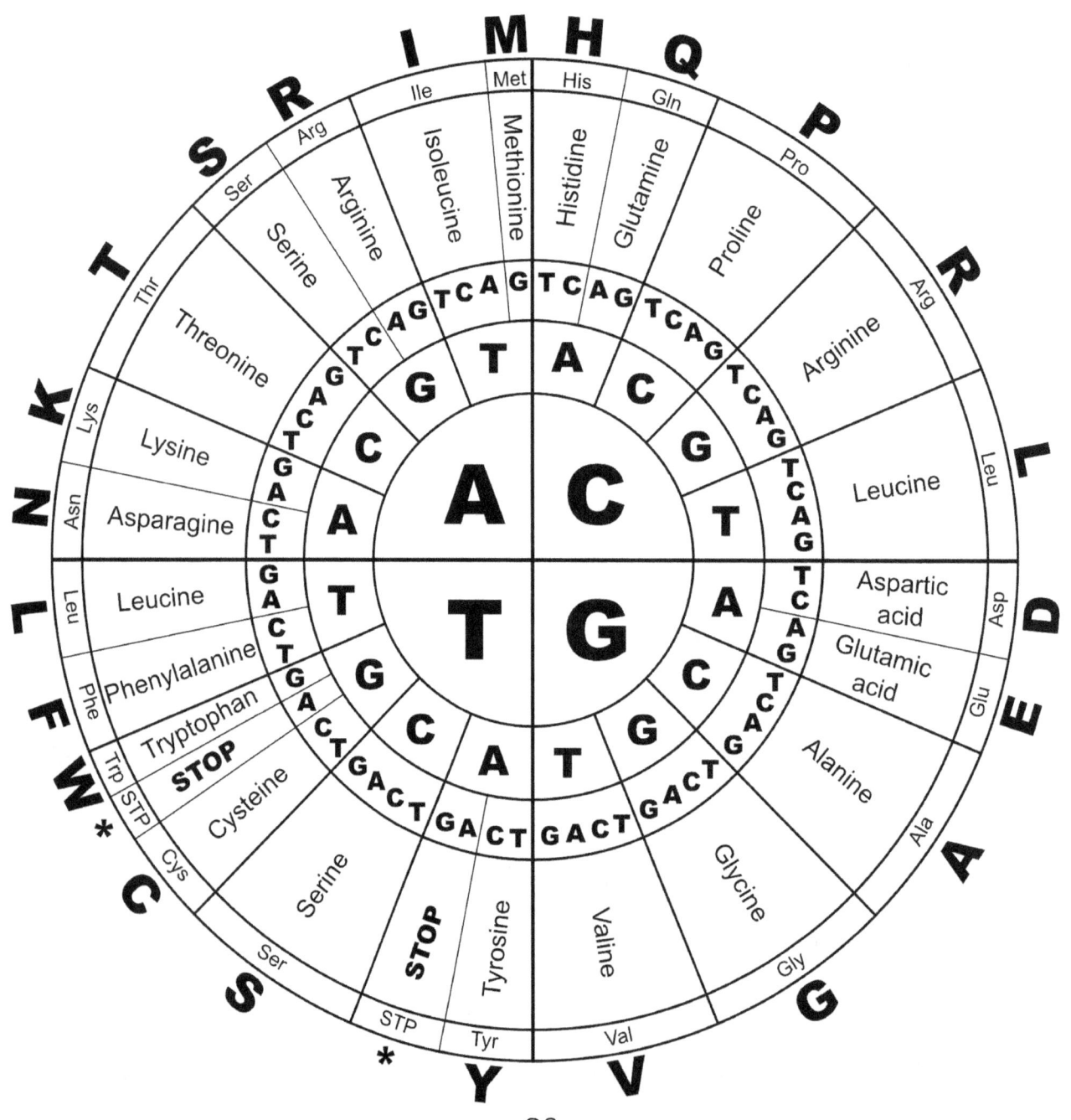

teins—occupy only about 2.5% of the human genome. Non-coding sequences make up the rest of it. Some of them may regulate when or how much certain genes are turned on, or help organize the genome inside the cell. Still others provide physical structures that serve another purpose, such as the repetitive sequences that make up the telomeres (ends) of chromosomes.

But much of the genome either has no specific function or serves a purpose that we haven't yet uncovered.

YOUR GENETIC DESTINY IS WRITTEN

GATTACA became one of my favorite science fiction movies long before I entered the field of genetics. It portrays a near-future dystopian society in which the worth and future potential of an individual are determined, at birth, with a genetic analysis. As a result, most parents take advantage of genetic selection/enhancement of embryos to get the ideal combination in their future child. These designer babies get the cool jobs, whereas babies born without such intervention are basically treated as invalids.

On the bright side, the idea of sequencing every person's genome at birth is rapidly becoming more plausible. Thanks to the advent of "next-generation" DNA sequencing technologies, we can now sequence a human genome in less than a week, for a little over a thousand dollars. We can use that information to infer a lot about a person, such as ancestry, risk for certain diseases, and likely physical appearance. But we're a long way off from predicting the lifetime risk for common diseases, like heart disease, diabetes, and psychiatric disorders.

Most of these result from complex interplay between genetic, lifestyle, and environmental factors. The vast majority of genetic variants associated with disease risk have a very small effect: they might increase your risk by 5%. There could be thousands of such genetic factors for any given disease, so predicting someone's health at birth, even if we knew everything about the genome, would be a very complex problem.

One thing I particularly admired about *GATTACA* was how the protagonist's genetic future was described in probabilities: neurological disorder, 60%; ADD, 89%; heart failure, 89%. There are few certainties in human genetics, and the movie did well to acknowledge this.

MUTATIONS ARE AWESOME

Mutations, or acquired changes in DNA, are one of the most misunderstood topics in genetics. Too often in science fiction, I see mutations treated as good or advantageous things. A telling example comes from the movie *Resident Evil*, in which the Red Queen (a sort of malicious AI in control of things) releases a genetically engineered monster that attacks the group of heroes. After it makes a kill, the Red Queen says that after it feeds, it will mutate, and then become something new. Presumably, an even stronger, deadlier monster.

The reality is that mutation, for humans at least, is uncommon. Most of the genetic variation that we have, we inherited from our parents. New mutations that arise in a child but are absent from both parents are extremely rare. We're talking about 40 or 50 throughout the entire genome, compared to 3 million inherited genetic variants.

Generally speaking, new mutations are not beneficial. The human genome has been under natural selection for thousands of years. Think of it like a Formula One racecar. Mutations are like metal screws that you add (or remove) at random. More than likely, this won't have any effect on the racecar, but if it does, you're far more likely to break something than to make it better.

The body's cells also acquire mutations over time, sometimes by chance as cells divide, but also through DNA damage induced by radiation or carcinogens. Most cells that suffer damaging mutations will die. Occasionally, however, a cell gets the right set of mutations that allow it to grow and divide uncontrollably. When this happens, cancer is the result.

GENETIC BLAME AND INEVITABILITY

I think that the most common myth about human genetics is that most traits are inherited in simple and/or inevitable fashion. The genetics taught in most high school biology classes—like dominant, recessive, and X-linked inheritance patterns—may be partially to blame for this. Mendel's laws and Punnett squares (remember those?) only work for rare genetic conditions that are due to mutations in a single gene. Cystic fibrosis and sickle-cell disease, for example, are recessive disorders caused by mutations in the CFTR and HBB genes, respectively.

Although Mendel's laws offer a useful introduction to genetic inheritance, they become problematic when we try to apply them to more complex traits. In fiction, I often meet characters living under a specter of a disease that killed their grandparents and/or parents. It seems inevitable that they, too, will fall victim to it.

Alcoholism, for example, is a complex disorder that's often treated simplistically: "My dad was an alcoholic, so I became one."

I'm sorry to have to tell you this, but most of the traits that make for interesting characters—intelligence, attractiveness, physical/mental health, etc.—do not follow simple laws of inheritance. They might not be passed from parent to child, or shared by siblings. The genetics underlying these characteristics will undoubtedly be complicated.

Just like we are.

Dan Koboldt is a genetics researcher and fantasy/science fiction author from the Midwest. He works for the Institute for Genomic Medicine at Nationwide Children's Hospital, where he and his colleagues use next-generation DNA sequencing technologies to uncover the genetic basis of pediatric diseases. He has co-authored more than 70 publications in *Nature*, *Science*, *The New England Journal of Medicine*, and other scientific journals.

Dan is also an avid hunter and outdoorsman. Every fall, he disappears into the woods to pursue whitetail deer and turkey with bow and arrow. He lives with his wife and three children in Ohio, where the deer take their revenge by eating all of the plants in his backyard.

FIVE QUESTIONS WITH THE EDITOR

JASON SIZEMORE

Q1

Why did you produce this print edition of your online zine?

ANSWER

It was time to produce a new sample issue to give out for promotions and contests. Apex has given away over 1,000 copies of the 2015 Sampler. I don't have any concrete data regarding whether having the sampler has helped boost our readership, but I do know that our authors and editors appreciate having a physical product they can handout at events.

Q2

Yeah, I get that. But this "sample" issue looks like a full-sized magazine. Isn't that a lot more work and cost to produce?

ANSWER

You're right. It is a lot more time and work. However, the dream is that there is sufficient reader interest to justify doing a quarterly print edition...perhaps a reboot of the old *Apex Science Fiction and Horror Digest.*

Q3

And that's why you're selling this for $7.99?

ANSWER

Yes.

Apex will still give away free copies for promotional reasons, but will be selling issue 0 at events this year to help offset costs and to gauge reader interest.

Q4

This issue is filled with reprints. If you do a new print edition will it have original work? Is this layout the look and feel we can expect in potential future issues?

ANSWER

That's two questions. Cheater.

The monthly content you see on Apex-Magazine.com would be collected and released quarterly in the print edition. The print edition with all three month's worth of content would be released before the content becomes available online.

I'm sure the layout will be refined and tweaked to look better over time. It's part of any publication's maturation process.

Q5

Why issue 0?

ANSWER

It's entirely possible (if not likely) that this is a one-shot. If a few years down the road I want to revisit the concept of a quarterly print publications, then I can still start at issue 1!

But mostly I've always wanted to do an issue 0 of something. It *feels* special. Now that the issue is finished, do I feel special? Always.